Time *for* Me *to* Come Home

Time *for* Me *to* Come Home

DOROTHY SHACKLEFORD
WITH TRAVIS THRASHER

NEW AMERICAN LIBRARY

New American Library
Published by the Penguin Group
Penguin Group (USA) LLC, 375 Hudson Street,
New York, New York 10014

USA | Canada | UK | Ireland | Australia | New Zealand | India | South Africa | China
penguin.com
A Penguin Random House Company

First published by New American Library,
a division of Penguin Group (USA) LLC

First Printing, November 2013

 REGISTERED TRADEMARK—MARCA REGISTRADA

LIBRARY OF CONGRESS CATALOGING-IN-PUBLICATION DATA:

Shackleford, Dorothy.
Time for Me to Come Home/Dorothy Shackleford, Travis Thrasher.
p. cm.
ISBN 978-0-451-46837-6 (hardback)
1. Families—Fiction. 2. Domestic fiction.
I. Thrasher, Travis, 1971– II. Title.
PS3619.H29T56 2013
813'.6—dc23   2013023731

Printed in the United States of America
3   5   7   9   10   8   6   4   2

Set in ITC Berkeley Book
Designed by Elke Sigal

It's funny how going back can get you back to
    where you belong
It's the difference between just a melody and my
    favorite Christmas song

> —"Time for Me to Come Home"
> by Dorothy Shackleford and Blake Shelton

This book is dedicated to all the people traveling
to get back home for Christmas, especially my children.

Time *for* Me
to Come Home

CHAPTER ONE

Here Comes Santa Claus

For a minute I forget what city I'm in.

I stare down at the Christmas tree in the plaza below my hotel window and realize I'm fried. It's one thing to forget where you're at if you're in the middle of the country, but you don't forget you're in New York City unless you've been on the road a long, *long* time.

It's late in Manhattan, and I don't have to leave anytime soon. I'm seriously thinking about spending Christmas in some tropical place. Like the Cayman Islands or maybe just some tiny little unnamed island where I can sip drinks with umbrellas swimming in them and I don't have to worry about anything, or talk to anyone.

Yeah, that'd be nice.

My head is still buzzing. It always does after shows, and not just from the noise onstage, but also from the energy of the crowd. It doesn't leave me for a while. Standing in front of twenty thousand people at Madison Square Garden can do that for you. Even if you're not the headliner. Seeing them singing the songs you wrote yourself, every single line, all in unison. It's impossible to simply turn off the switch and try to go to sleep. Or try to do anything, really.

I swallow a couple of aspirin and place the bottled water on the window ledge. The headache is coming and I'm needing something to just help stabilize this crazy ride. A ride that's finally going to stop and take a break.

The Gunslingers Tour hit the road with forty-two dates, all sold out with crowds ready to party. It was billed as a double-barrel shotgun with Heath Sawyer and Sean Torrent. It was a gamble to begin with, pairing a country artist with a rock star, not to mention a rising star like me partnered with a superstar making his comeback. I was the middle act performing before Torrent, which was a great opportunity for me. Somehow, managers and agents and labels managed to make it work, all because they smelled money. Once we started making good money with a dozen shows, they added thirty more including Madison Square Garden.

I think about what they were going to initially call the tour. The Good, the Bad, and the Ugly Tour. I would've been the good guy with my latest album called *Two Guns*. Sean, the notorious rock star who finally got clean and released his album *Comeback Kid*, would've been the bad guy (and the true headliner). But nobody wanted to be labeled ugly (especially since the opening act was a set of beautiful twin ladies in a band called the Nixx). So we went with the Gunslingers Tour, a nice thing since it was an obvious nod to my record.

I should be celebrating with the band and the label and the hangers-on I just left partying downstairs, but I'm too tired. Not just a need-a-vacation sort of tired but an epic end-of-the-world sort of tired. The kind that produces a lot of zombies. The kind of tired a soul might never come back from.

The best way I can sum up my mood is it's like someone threw me out of a plane, yet in the middle of plummeting toward the ground below I feel like drifting off to sleep. I'm a Jekyll and Hyde of energy and emotion.

I spend some time looking at the online buzz about the concert on my laptop. Then I close it and wipe my tired eyes.

Wonder what they'd think if I shared what I'm really thinking about this holiday?

But there's no place for honesty, for being awash in melancholy. That's a different genre. My world won't allow for that. My songs and my persona don't go there. A musician like Sean Torrent can, but not me. Normally I don't go there, but it's the end of the tour, and those little demons of doubt are starting to remind me that eventually my time's gonna be up. I'll finally reach the ground again. The spotlight will shine on someone else. It always does.

Ho ho ho boo freaking hoo.

The party is still raging, and maybe I'll go back downstairs to the bar to join them. But something in me wants to be alone. It's time to tell the gang good-bye. Winter has come and I gotta go hibernate. The music still gets played, but music makers retreat, at least for a while. To write new songs. To devise new strategies and tours. Or maybe just to sleep.

Or maybe to go back home, especially when you've been gone far too long.

I finish off my water and think I need something a little stronger. Then I hear my phone go off. It plays a familiar song. It's my manager. I just saw him but didn't say good night. He probably is wondering if his cash cow got run over outside by a reindeer.

I let it go to voice mail. It's one o'clock here in the Big Apple. Most people are asleep, dreaming of the next few days, when they'll see their families and open gifts and eat lots of home-cooked meals and celebrate the Christmas season. But not the music business. The heart of that business keeps beating, morning, noon, and night.

And all they want is more, especially when the public is clamoring for it.

For a moment I don't want to think about the business. I don't want to think about my label and the next album they're already wanting me to get to work on (not to mention the Christmas album I'm supposed to nail down details on). I don't want to listen to the demos they've sent me or attempt to think of song titles myself.

All I want for Christmas is silence. And maybe the comfort of a pretty stranger.

A minute passes, and the phone goes off again. I go to pick it up, a bit annoyed and ready to ask Sam what's going on. But the ringtone is different.

"It's Gotta Be Someone" begins to play. I should know, since it's one of my songs. It's actually my momma's favorite song of mine.

There's gotta be something wrong.

"Momma?"

There's no reason she should be calling this late.

"Heath?"

"Momma, are you okay?"

"I'm fine."

"What are you still doing up?"

"You're up, aren't you?"

I hear that familiar drawl that instantly makes me feel like a kid living in Okmulgee, Oklahoma, again. It doesn't matter if I'm thirty-five. It doesn't matter if I'm a guy just on the cusp of breaking out big-time. It will never matter, since the voice on the other line will always be Momma. The woman who carried me in her belly for nine months. The only one in the world who will always have my heart no matter how many times I break hers.

"How'd the show go?"

"It was amazing. Really one of the best."

"You sound tired."

Strangely, Momma doesn't. "What's going on? Is everybody okay?"

"It's time for you to come home, Heath."

For a moment I'm silent. And I'm never silent. But I don't know what to say.

"We're all waiting for you."

I might be thinking a lot of things, and have lots of plans, but there's nothing I can really say except the obvious. "I was plannin' on coming home."

This is a lie. I wasn't planning anything. I had been debating and procrastinating and rationalizing, but, nope, I sure wasn't planning anything. Except, of course, stealing away to a tropical paradise.

I love my Oklahoma, but it's not exactly what I'd call a tropical paradise.

"They all want to see you," Momma tells me, which really means *she* wants to see me.

"Man, it's been wild," I say as I start to sum up how busy I've been on the tour. But the truth is I've been avoiding confirming whether I was going to come home for Christmas. Now I can't put it off anymore.

"It'll be good for you," Momma says.

I haven't been home in a long while. What Momma refers to as being good for me is probably the thing I've been most avoiding.

We talk for a few more minutes, but this is what Momma called me for. This is what she's been calling me for all day. There is only one answer she wanted and probably expected.

"I'll be there soon," I say.

"Hurry home," she tells me before saying good-bye.

I know I'm stuck now, since I've said for sure that I'm coming home. It's been easy to be busy and to tell her I wasn't sure what was happening. But I just told her I'd be coming home.

Wonderful.

"I expect some good gifts," I joke before getting off the phone.

Momma just tells me good night and says she loves me. I agree with her. It's been a good night, and I know she loves me. I just have no idea how she knows that I'm tired and restless, and that I need to come home.

I hold the empty water bottle in my hand and start to squeeze the plastic. Then I let out an obnoxious sigh, playing up my exhaustion for the empty hotel room. I turn up the television and listen to the Christmas music playing and wonder why I'm so Grinch-like. I don't want any chestnuts and I don't want any Jack Frost and I really, truly don't want any Yuletide carols.

You're a big fat turkey, aren't you?

Maybe I won't go home after all. I can find an excuse. I hear there are storms coming. Sure—I can use that one. Or a dozen others. I don't want to go back home because I don't want to go back to being that guy when that guy hasn't been around for a long time.

The scary thing, if I have to be honest, is I don't really know the new guy who replaced the old one. I wouldn't recognize him if I saw him on the street or heard him singing some number one hit song. And I bet I don't particularly like him much, either.

In my dream that night, I hear Elvis telling me here comes Santa Claus. But this isn't a dream, really. It's a nightmare. I see not just one Santa but a whole troop of them coming down Santa Claus Lane. And like a kid stuck on the freeway in rush hour traffic, I have nowhere to go. I can't get out of their way. I see their thick beards and plump bellies and round eyes, and meanwhile Elvis is sounding like Elvis doing bad Elvis-karaoke.

I wake up and I'm sweating. Maybe this is what happens when you substitute M&M's for dinner. Or when you fall asleep watching *A Christmas Story*.

I know I need to get home.

I need a break. I need Momma. I need a place I know better than myself.

I open my laptop and book a flight leaving tomorrow afternoon, the earliest possible. I haven't booked a flight for myself in a long time.

Sleep doesn't come again for a while. I wonder who's going to be singing the next Christmas lullaby in my dreams. Burl Ives? Bing Crosby?

Another song starts to form instead. This is one I've been hearing for a while. I still need to let it out, to finally get it out of my head. But I'm afraid to start writing that song.

I don't want to go there. Not now. Not yet.

'Cause I still don't know how to truly say good-bye.

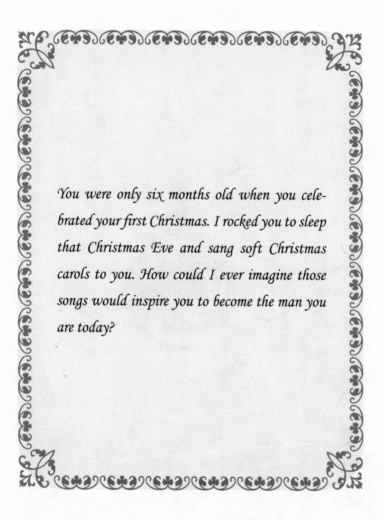

You were only six months old when you celebrated your first Christmas. I rocked you to sleep
that Christmas Eve and sang soft Christmas
carols to you. How could I ever imagine those
songs would inspire you to become the man you
are today?

CHAPTER TWO

Home for the Holidays

I'm washing my hands in the men's bathroom at LaGuardia when I see a woman rush in and find an available stall. For a second I think I'm seeing things. I stare for a moment as water drips onto my pants. I see other guys coming and going, but the blonde dressed in a light khaki business suit just sweeps into the john and doesn't seem to know she's in the wrong bathroom. Or maybe she just doesn't care. As she tries to shut the door with her large shoulder bag blocking it, I notice a dark brown streak splashed across the front of the almost cream-colored blazer.

That's not a spill. That looks like a protest movement.

I wait there, amused. I want to see her look when she comes back out and realizes where she's at. This'll be something fun to tell my family about when I get back home.

I hear an exasperated sigh from the stall, and I see her heels moving about. It looks like she's changing. A stranger stops and tells me he loves my latest album. I nod and smile and thank him. Soon I see the door open up and see the woman's face look around. Her hair seems windblown and wavy, like she forgot to finish the job when getting ready this morning. Wide eyes stare as she pauses on the way to the sinks. A few men laugh, including me.

"When you gotta go, you gotta go," she says as she steps beside me and washes her hands.

She's wearing the most hideous Christmas sweater I've ever seen. It's got both Santa Claus and Rudolph sewn onto it and sticking out, along with some ornaments and glitter and other stuff. It looks like a dog ate the Christmas decorations in the house, then threw up on this multicolored sweater.

This is when I know I'm being pranked by someone.

"That's a good one," I tell her. "If you wanted a picture, all you needed to do was ask."

Of course, I'm teasing, because I know a camera somewhere in the restroom is filming me.

She smiles at me through the mirror and keeps washing her hands. "I'm good. Thanks, though."

Her eyes aren't just blue—they're bright and announce themselves like exclamation points. Just like her god-awful sweater. The glance she gives me is strange, because I haven't seen that sort of a glance for a while. It's the kind I used to get when people didn't know my name. The kind I had when strangers regarded me the same way I regarded them.

There's something in her tone that tells me she doesn't want to talk about it.

But it's gotta be a joke, right? This whole thing, including her ridiculous sweater. That can't be real.

Yet everything about her gives off the seriously annoyed vibe. I simply nod and smile, then start to walk away, but the woman calls out to me.

"You forgot your phone."

I smile and shake my head. "I'm good, but thanks."

It's an arrogant reply, but I'm just havin' a little fun. Until I feel my jeans pocket and realize she's right. I must have put my phone on the counter before washing my hands.

She picks it up and examines the camo cover. "I like your style."

I can tell she's mocking me from the wry grin on her face. I bet she's vegetarian anyway, since she doesn't seem to have an ounce of fat on her bones. She hands me the phone and I nod.

"You owe me," she says, smiles in a strange way, then walks out of the bathroom wearing heels and dress pants along with the winner of the worst-Christmas-sweater-ever contest.

Did this girl recognize me or what?

If she did, then suddenly I think I'm in love. Not really, because she's cute in that girl-next-door sort of way. Generally I go for someone a little more exotic. Someone a little more curvy. But something in that spunk and in those eyes . . . They amuse me.

If she didn't recognize me, then I'm some dude she just met in the bathroom gawking at her and carrying a phone with a camo cover. I bought it for more of a joke, so people can think I'm a bona fide hunter when I'm talking on my iPhone.

I'm not a bona fide anything, unless it's jokester.

I have some time to kill in the lounge, and I plan to do exactly that. I should've waited to use the bathroom there. Then I wouldn't have looked like a moron trying to pick up a chick in an ugly sweater in the men's bathroom.

*   *   *

Turns out, the airline lounge is closed for repairs. That makes sense, since nobody is traveling at this time of the year. You know—since it's only December 23. It's nice that they put some Christmas ribbon on the doors and a sign wishing me a Merry Christmas.

I find a grill and get a booth in the back. It's not that I don't love seeing people, especially fans. The problem is I can end up spending an hour talking to strangers when all I really want to do is grab a beer and answer some e-mail that's several days old. The booth gives me a little privacy. If this was down south or back home in Oklahoma, forget about it. But since this is New York, there are a lot of people who just don't care. They might recognize me, but they're far too busy to actually come up and say something. That's why I love New York. Couldn't live here, but love visiting.

I'm squinting at my iPhone, since it's dark in this grill, when my theory about being left alone gets proven wrong.

"You could read a lot better if you tried on some glasses."

I turn and see the woman from the bathroom standing at the end of the bar, with her blue eyes and amused grin. Her hair doesn't look as wild, and she's wearing a jacket over the Christmas sweater, but I can still see Santa popping out like some Peeping Tom.

"It's dark in here," I tell her.

"I've seen you squinting at that thing for the last ten minutes."

She doesn't sound like a ditz. She sounds tough, like a woman used to getting things done.

"Are you following me?" I ask, again half joking.

"I'm waiting for a table."

The seat across from me suddenly seems to shout out like a grade-school kid asking a teacher to pick him. Yet I already made things awkward enough back in the men's room. I don't want to push it.

"You might be waiting a while," I say, since nothing else really comes to mind.

"See—that was your chance to say 'Hey, there's an empty seat right across from me. Would you like to sit there?' I'm already having the best day of my life."

She has a feisty little smile on her face. It's cute. And a little crazy.

"My wife might not like that."

"I didn't see a wedding ring," she says.

"You looked, huh?"

"It was obvious when you grabbed your phone."

She talks in a matter-of-fact sort of way, not in a flirty or suggestive manner. I honestly don't have any idea if she really wants to sit across from me. Or even if she knows who I am.

"You can sit down if you want to."

"Okay. Thanks. Such a gentleman."

She slides in and puts her purse down next to her, then brushes back her hair and smiles. "I'm Cara."

"Heath."

I shake her hand and can't stop smiling, thinking someone put her up to this. Or someone's messing with me. I look around for a moment.

"What is it?" She looks sincere and honest in her question.

I don't want to ask the obvious.

Wait. You don't know who I am? How dare you? I'm the great and mighty Heath Sawyer and you must've been living in a cave not to know who I am after the year I've had!

I know how full of myself that would sound. But still—I just can't help but think one of the guys is messing around.

"Did Pete put you up to this?"

Cara's eyes look puzzled. "Pete who?"

"You don't know any Pete?"

"Should I know a Pete? What are you talking about?"

Just say it. Go ahead and say it. You can't help yourself.

I laugh instead.

"Am I missing something?"

"No, I think you have just about everything there on your sweater," I tell her.

She shakes her head and sighs, and I don't get any sort of sense that the sweater is a joke.

"Can you explain a bit?" I ask.

"Some moron in his fancy suit was talking on his phone and carrying a venti Starbucks and plowed right into me. He literally poured half of it all over me. He apologized, like, for five seconds, then said he was late for his flight. Another typical guy I have to clean up after."

I nod. "Yeah, that sucks. Sorry about that. But . . ."

"What?" she asks, annoyed that I'm prying.

"What's the scoop with the sweater?"

"What, this?" Cara takes off her jacket and then examines the sweater. "You don't love this?"

She bobbles Santa and Rudolph in a funny sort of way.

"I'd pay big money for that," I tell her.

"My brother gave it to me. We exchange awful Christmas

sweaters every year, and he gave it to me before dropping me off at the airport."

"Ah, so—"

"So it was the only thing I had available. It was either going to be the coffee stain or the hideous sweater."

"Tough choice," I say. "So where are you from?"

"Tulsa."

Now I really do laugh out loud. "Come on."

"What?"

"Did I need to introduce myself?"

For a moment, Cara studies me, then seems to get what I'm saying. At least I think she does.

"Do we know each other? Are you from Tulsa?"

"Do you ever listen to the radio?" I ask.

She nods. A server comes and takes her order. She orders a BLT sandwich without the B or the mayo. She asks what kind of diet soda they have, then decides she prefers a water. She also asks if they have any aspirin.

Okay, so she's not a ditz, but she's high maintenance.

"I love listening to the radio," she says.

"You do, huh? So who do you like?"

"I'm a big Maroon Five fan. Love their last album. And Rihanna."

"How about country?"

"Country music? Ugh. Can't stand it."

I nod. Now I *know* someone put her up to this. Maybe even paid her. "Yeah, me too. I just hate all that twang and songs about drinking and shacking up."

"And dating your cousins," Cara says.

"And fixing fence posts. And killing deer."

"All my friends can't get enough of the stuff. Doesn't help where we live."

"No, it doesn't."

I wait for her to say more, but she doesn't.

She might not have any idea who you are.

I don't buy it. Even non–country music fans read *People* magazine. Or watch the television. So I'll play along. I like a good old-fashioned gag.

I notice a text coming in and pick up my phone. Again, it takes me a while to read it.

"Here," Cara says as she digs into her purse. "Try these out."

The little glasses might snap if I put them on my big head. "Those might not fit."

"They cost a buck. They're just reading glasses."

"I don't need reading glasses."

She puts them in my hand. One thing this woman happens to be is forceful.

"Fine." I slip them on and the text I was reading comes to life like a 3-D movie. I take them off as if they're infected with the plague.

"It worked, huh?"

"No."

"Yeah, they did. Don't lie. They're low dose. I only use them when I'm reading."

"It's just 'cause it's dark in here."

"It's not *that* dark," Cara says.

I fold them up and give them back to her. "I think I'm good, *thanks*."

She laughs at me echoing her comment in the bathroom.

So far she hasn't said a word about wandering into the men's restroom. Maybe she doesn't think it's that big of a deal.

"So where are you headed to today?"

"Tulsa, just like you."

She looks surprised. "Really? You live there?"

"I used to. Now I live in Nashville."

"Going home for the holidays?"

I nod slowly, then look around again. I guess I can't help the smirk on my face.

"Okay—what?" Cara says. "Am I missing something?"

Yeah. A lot.

"No."

"So why the grin and the looks around like I'm missing some kind of joke? Was it that funny that I went into the men's bathroom? Or is it the sweater?"

"You didn't see the sign?"

"Uh, no."

For a moment, Cara looks serious and sober. Almost . . . sad. I go to say something and then she beats me to it.

"Look, I just wanted to grab a bite to eat before the flight. It's been a long couple of days."

Just as I'm about try again, I see the name on my phone. I might have a hard time reading texts and news, but I can see this name very clearly.

I can't take this conversation in front of a stranger. Regardless of whether she's playing a prank on me or not.

I answer and say, "Hey, give me a minute, okay?"

Then I stand and reach into my wallet. I put a couple of twenties on the table.

"I'm sorry—I have to take this."

She puts up a hand and shakes her head. "No, no. Please—you can stay here and talk—"

"It's fine. I was getting ready to go anyway."

Cara looks a bit embarrassed, and once again I think, *She really has no clue who I am*. That's okay.

The woman on the other end of this phone knows who I am. She knows too well.

She knows Heath Sawyer, the country music jerk who broke her heart.

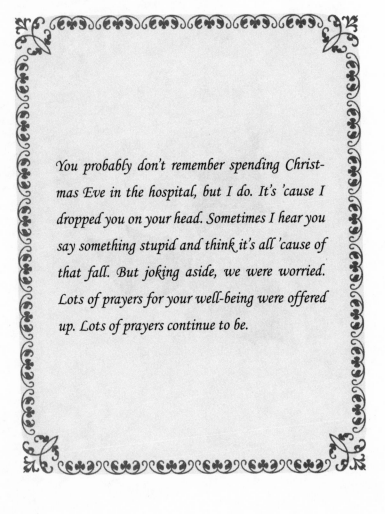

You probably don't remember spending Christmas Eve in the hospital, but I do. It's 'cause I dropped you on your head. Sometimes I hear you say something stupid and think it's all 'cause of that fall. But joking aside, we were worried. Lots of prayers for your well-being were offered up. Lots of prayers continue to be.

CHAPTER THREE

Don't Shoot Me, Santa

"*I* should be going home with you."

Naomi still doesn't get it. This is part of her problem.

"You shouldn't be going home with me because we're not together," I say into the phone as I stand in an empty terminal gate and try to avoid being seen.

"Why do you hate me so much?"

I laugh. I never know what I'm going to get with good ol' Naomi. Today it's the victim. Tomorrow it might be a viper.

"I don't hate you. I just think—no, I know—we shouldn't be together."

"I love you."

"You love the fame and fortune. What happens when it's all gone?"

"I want you, Heath."

"The last time we talked, you said you wanted to castrate me."

"I was angry." Naomi's voice is soft and timid. She should've been an actress.

"No, no, no," I say. "Normal people get angry. You go postal. I mean, seriously, girl. You probably forgot half the things you said to me on the phone."

"I was angry."

"Being with you is a full-time job. Not to mention that it feels like going off to war."

She pauses for a minute. I can see her beautiful face and round lips looking all sad like some expensive Chihuahua adorned in jewelry and fancy clothes.

"Why do you want to hurt me?"

"I want to help you. The longer we stay together, the more likely someone will die."

"Stop it."

"I'm just bein' honest."

"You're teasing."

"I'm not jokin' around, Naomi. You're kinda like the devil. It's all fun and games until I see the flames around me and re- alize I'm right outside of hell's gate."

"That hurts."

"Do you remember getting the scissors and cutting my jeans? That's crazyland. And you want me to bring you home? Girl, I gotta tell you—"

"I'll never love anybody the way I love you."

I chuckle. *Man, this girl is dangerous.* I'd be suckered back in, too, if I saw her in person. It's just that way with Naomi.

"That's so touching and heartfelt," I joke.

She calls me a familiar name that's not so flattering. When she's not trying to take me back or giving me clichéd love talk on the phone, she's usually cursing my name and every part of my body.

"I could've just ignored your call," I tell her.

"Then why didn't you?"

"'Cause I want the best for you. I really do."

"You're the best for me."

"That I know isn't true. This last year—tell me it's been fun."

"It's been fun," she says.

We met each other a year and a half ago. The courting process was fun. Once we actually started dating and became official, it turned into a train wreck. Naomi lost herself in the bright lights and the big city.

Maybe that's the only thing she wanted in the first place.

"It's not been fun. It's been a lot of work. Then it got to a point where it was actually totally and completely dysfunctional. I've said this before—Dr. Clarence is a good doctor—"

She hangs up on me. It's not like I'm telling her to visit a shrink I've never seen before. He's a good guy and I think he can really help a head case like Naomi.

I recall all the times we'd argue half a day away. All the wasted hours, for what? All the wasted time, for what exactly?

Well, there was all that.

Naomi was a lot of fun. She was like a spring break going on all year, always up for drinks and a night out to see and be seen, always high energy and ready for more. That just doesn't work 24/7. Eventually you need to go back to reality. Eventually you need to go back home and start living a normal life again.

I shut off my phone and don't try to call her back. I was just hoping I could make a little more peace. And this is a little better than how we left off last time. A little.

On my way to the gate, I see a Santa Claus sitting on the floor, leaning against the wall, waiting for a flight that's delayed. What an odd sight. I have to go ask him for a picture that I can send to some of my bandmates. When I do, he looks up at me with glassy eyes.

"What part about sitting down minding my own business makes it look like I want to get my picture taken?"

We have an angry Santa here. Even better for the photo.

"Come on, man. Just one photo."

"Oh, let me think about it . . . No."

I'm having a lot of good fortune here in the airport today.

"Aren't you supposed to be exhausted the day *after* Christmas?" I ask him.

"You're that country singer, aren't you?"

Recognizing me doesn't seem to make his mood any better. He says this like I burned down his barn.

"Heath Sawyer," I say, offering to shake his hand.

"Man, I hated your last album," he says, ignoring my gesture.

It seems Santa is a little tipsy.

"Sorry to hear that."

"No country singer should ever have a rapper on his album."

Obviously Santa has me confused with somebody else. I nod and look for my gate number.

"Whoa, whoa, hold on," Santa says as he stands up on unsteady feet. "Let's get that picture."

His breath reeks of Mardi Gras instead of Christmas.

"Too much eggnog?" I ask as I take a picture of us.

"You try dressing up like this and roaming around the airport when there are delays. It's brutal."

"The kids gotta love it."

"Oh, yeah, they love it. I'm a human piñata—that's what I am. It's no longer about asking what they want for Christmas. It's about being asked when I'm going to get a real job."

"You from New York?"

Santa looks at me with a *Where do you think I'm from?* sort of glance. "Uh, yeah. Where are you headed to?"

"Tulsa."

Santa only laughs. "Man, no flight headed west is gonna make it. You watch the weather report?"

"Not really."

"Want to borrow my suit? You might have a lot of time to kill."

"How long have you been wearing it?" I joke.

"Too long," he says, then adding to my horror, "I'm not wearing anything underneath the Santa outfit. No T-shirt, nothing."

"Thanks, buddy. If my plane goes down, I know what I'll be thinking about before I die."

This finally gets a laugh, which I'm grateful for. If he had his hand out asking for money, I'd give it to him. But now I have a feeling he'd punch me in the face if I gave him anything. I nod and wish him a Merry Christmas.

"The only merry thing coming my way is a bottle of Jack."

"Tell him I say hi. I know him well."

"Forget the rappers on your next album," Santa tells me. "Why don't you do a Christmas album? Everybody's doing one."

"I've been talking about doing one. We'll see."

"No rappers."

"Got it."

I still don't know who he's talking about, but I know it's not me. As I begin to walk away, Kris Kringle shouts behind me, "You're not getting home before Christmas!"

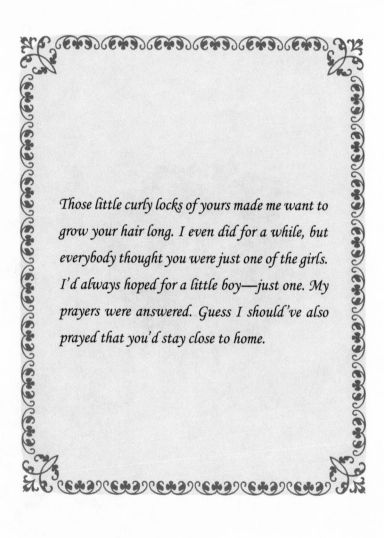

Those little curly locks of yours made me want to grow your hair long. I even did for a while, but everybody thought you were just one of the girls. I'd always hoped for a little boy—just one. My prayers were answered. Guess I should've also prayed that you'd stay close to home.

CHAPTER FOUR

Do You Hear What I Hear?

The flight to Tulsa has been canceled. Now the only way to get home is by going through Chicago O'Hare. Momma told me there's a nasty storm hovering around the middle of the country, exactly where I'm headed. The new flight I'm on has been delayed a couple of hours. Fortunately, I'm able to get some things done, thanks to my wonderful smartphone. Not sure how anybody got anything done before the invention of these personal computers built for the palm of your hand and your thumb.

I used to think success equaled taking life easy. I didn't know that once you step this high on that fame-and-fortune ladder, it takes a ton of work to stay up here. Becoming a household name brings a host of responsibilities, expectations, and issues to deal with. I've accepted this, and in no way would I ever begin to complain, since this is the life I'd wanted. But still—sometimes I just want to shut off the Heath Sawyer switch and relax a bit. If I did that, though, someone somewhere would surely be more than happy to switch places and deal with the "struggles" of being me.

My mind is always making mental to-do lists for my career. Right now, I can think of several glaring issues that I want to deal with. I don't want to wait, because those who wait usually pay the price for doing so.

There's the issue of my guitarist, who officially called it quits after our show at Madison Square Garden last night. His last words were something to the effect that he'd rather shave his head and beard and become a monk than ever play the guitar for me again. I think he just needs to go home and get some sleep like the rest of us. But then again, he might be warming up his electric razor.

There's the benefit show that's scheduled for the same night as an award show and somehow I managed to say yes to both. I'll have to rebook the benefit show by doing something even bigger and better.

There's discussion of the pros and cons of recording a Christmas album. I've already agreed to do one, but before I can commit to doing something so clichéd, I need to narrow down tracks. My iPod is loaded with five hundred of the best Christmas songs ever. I think I have about twenty-five versions of "Silent Night" waiting to be listened to. Classic versions. Funny versions (funny meaning poorly done).

I've already received four e-mails today from my record label. All different ways of talking about the next album. It hasn't even been twenty-four hours since the last concert ended and they're already talking about a new record.

One e-mail says:

> Let's start talking about studio time after the holidays.

Another e-mail says:

> You gotta hear this new Sparkland & Winter demo—
> it's like it was written just for you.

> Wondering if there's any chance the new album could
> come out before the ACM awards in April.

Sure, I think. *Let's sell an album and a hundred-venue tour and then focus on writing and recording the songs later.*

There are Oklahoma issues I need to figure out—selling the house or keeping it. Tax issues that I'd rather be beaten to a pulp than have to actually decide on. Brand management issues and future touring issues and background singer issues, and then there's the matter of the fan/stalker/weirdo guy making up things on my Facebook page.

Eventually I stop thinking about all of this and continue to see what fans are saying online. This is the fun stuff, sometimes the only stuff that keeps me going. It's the fans. Man, I know that's Pop Star Talk 101, but it's true. The fans help me keep whatever sanity I have left while the business tries to slowly suck it away. I continue messing around on my smartphone until we start boarding and I'm in my first-class window seat like always. It's not very long before I see those blue eyes walking through the doorway of the plane. Cara sees me and instantly smiles.

"Well, at least we're heading halfway home," she says as the line pauses and she stands next to the attendant's station.

"If we even get off the ground," I say, probably jinxing us all with that comment.

The seat to my left is empty and for a second I know she's going to sit there. She's going to sit down and talk my ear off and there's no way I'll be able to get rid of her . . .

But she says, "Enjoy the flight," and keeps shuffling past.

Soon I have my earbuds in and I'm listening to some Christmas songs. A businessman sits down beside me in his expensive tailored suit, and I think what it would have been like having his life. Working for a machine and constantly selling something and worrying about the bottom line and the boss . . .

Are you talking about the businessman or yourself?

We're not that different, if I'm honest. The music matters—it still means something. But at the end of the day, it's about a brand and a business. I'm the smiling spokesperson who happens to be pretty good playing a guitar and keeping a melody. But I'm still selling something. Something a lot of people are buying.

I remember something my father told me early in my career: "Don't ever forget why you're doing this. Don't ever forget the great privilege you have. The great gift. 'Cause there's gonna be plenty—plenty—of people who are gonna come across your path who're interested in one thing and one thing only."

On the Christmas song I'm listening to, Bing Crosby asks, "Do you hear what I hear?"

Yep, I hear it. It's the jingle jangle of the Christmas season, of the cash register, of the clanking of coins.

It's the one thing and one thing only that my father warned me about. I wonder how well I've done heeding it.

About an hour into the flight, while the businessman beside me is in the first-class bathroom, I decide to walk to the back of the plane. I can justify it by saying that I really have to go or that I just want to stretch my legs, but maybe there's another reason, too. Maybe I'll get a chance to see someone and say hi.

Even though half the plane's gonna notice who you are.

The two drinks I just had make me feel warm walking down the center aisle. I pass Cara, who is sitting in a window seat near the back of the plane, looking out while bobbing her head to the music playing through her headphones. Nobody is sitting next to her. I hear the pulsing beat and wonder what she's listening to. Nothing of mine, I know. I don't have that many beats a minute in any song I've ever done. This body might have some soul in it, but these feet sure don't dance.

I'm washing my hands in the bathroom when the plane decides to drop, like, ten thousand feet. For a second I feel like I'm free-falling—everything suddenly becomes light and my stomach and brain all stay up high while the rest of me drops low. I hang on to the sink and then feel the plane trying to sort things out like a stomach does after you've eaten some really bad Mexican food. Everything shudders and I suddenly get woozy.

My hands are still wet when I open the door. The plane is

bouncing, and all I can think about is that opening episode of *Lost* when the plane tore apart in three pieces and people in the back were simply ripped out into the bright, blue sky—

Stop it and get to a seat.

The first empty seat I spot is the one next to the stranger I keep running into. I get to the seat and strap myself in. She looks up and smiles. The vibrating bouncing jerking starts again, so I don't even think again. Cara's music is still pounding away like a Jay-Z concert. She slips off the headphones, but the tune continues.

"You okay?" she asks.

"Yeah," I say, wiping sweat off my forehead.

She laughs. "You're white as a ghost. Don't like turbulence?"

"Not a big fan, no," I say. "That and tiny dogs. Hate 'em both."

It suddenly feels like someone's shaking the entire plane, like a toddler pounding away on a toy. I grip the armrests as the woman next to me watches me.

"We're fine. I've felt worse."

"That doesn't mean I have to like it. "

"Settle down. It's gonna be okay." She pats my leg as she says this.

This woman makes me feel like a fifth grader. And she's the teacher.

I nod and sigh.

"Seriously, Heath, we're gonna be okay."

"The rational part of me agrees with you, but I just—"

Suddenly the plane starts heading straight down into a death spiral, the ground beneath us surely getting closer and closer until the plane makes a giant, fiery crater inside it.

The shaking continues, but I can feel that we're not exactly going straight down. Even if it feels that way when my eyes are closed.

I feel a hand take mine. I open my eyes and see those blue eyes looking at me with sympathy now.

"Just look at me. It's going to be okay."

I glance at her and see something I haven't spotted before. This genuine and tender look of care on her face. Not the admiration of a fan or a starstruck awe in her eyes, but just simple concern.

"We're going to be fine," she continues.

There's an innocence to Cara that I don't spot a lot these days. An innocence that seems strangely out of tune with the song I hear coming from her headphones.

"Is that Prince?" I ask.

She nods.

The last person in the world I'd expect to be listening to Prince is Cara.

"Is that 'When Doves Cry'?"

"Yeah. Love Prince. Michael Jackson too."

The turbulence starts in again, but this time it doesn't bother me as much. I'm more amused than anything.

"You don't strike me as the Prince type."

"Too goody-goody-looking?"

"Too something," I say.

She turns off the song and then puts the headphones in her lap.

"I love to dance."

"I couldn't dance to save my life," I say.

The bouncing and jerking of the flight have stopped now.

But that doesn't mean I'm ready to take off my seat belt and move back up the aisle. Cara doesn't seem to be bothered that I'm sitting next to her.

For a second I notice her hideous sweater again. But somehow, it doesn't look *that* bad anymore. Somehow it looks kinda cute. Just like Cara.

I'm getting altitude sickness and it's going to my head.

"So what kind of music do you like?" Cara asks. "You said you liked country, right?"

She really doesn't recognize me. This is amusing. Not because I think every single person out there should recognize me. But because of the conversations we've had, eventually she might end up realizing who she's talking to and suddenly feel stupid.

Or maybe she won't. Maybe it won't mean a thing to her. I mean—it's not like I'm Prince suddenly sitting down beside her.

"I love hipster bands."

"No, you don't," she says.

"No, I do. The tighter the jeans, the better the band."

"You're just joking."

I chuckle and nod. "Tell me—what is it about tight jeans on a guy? What guy in his right mind would ever put some on and think they look good? I mean—really?"

"You'd never wear tight jeans?"

"I'd like to have children one day."

"No children now?"

"None that I know of," I joke.

"Here, look," she says, digging through her purse to find her phone. She touches it to find something. "There's my baby."

I'm assuming she's going to show me a picture of a dog or

even—God forbid—a cat. I've known plenty of ladies that have been gaga over animals. I love animals, but they're not my children and never will be.

When she leans the screen toward me, I see a picture of a baby boy. He's looking up at the camera and reaching toward it. His cheeks look like two giant helium-filled balloons. He looks like the happiest kid in the world. He also looks like he eats nothing but donuts.

"That's Andrew."

I know she said she's not married. Or did she say that? I don't see a ring.

"I can see the questions on your face," Cara says, laughing. "That's my nephew. My sister's son."

"He's cute. Looks like trouble. Does your sister live in New York City?"

"No, she's in Tulsa. I had an accounting seminar in the city."

Ah, that explains it.

"What?" Cara asks.

"So I bet you're ready to get home and spoil your nephew rotten."

"Yeah. You could say that."

There's more to this woman than what she's saying or how she's smiling.

"So you think we'll make it home?" she says.

I shrug. "The weather's getting nasty. That's what my momma said."

"Your whole family back in Oklahoma?"

"Yep. It's the first Christmas without my father. I have three sisters, so—so, yeah, I need to get back home and take care of the ladies, including Momma. Or have 'em take care of me."

"Been around Chicago much?"

"How come?" I ask.

"Well, who knows? You might be spending Christmas there."

"There are worse places to be."

"Any place is worse if you're not home with your family."

The plane has steadied and the pilot announces that we're going to be descending for our landing soon.

"Thanks for holding my hand," I tell Cara.

"I'm good at that."

"Holding strangers' hands?"

"Oh, come on. We go way back. Plus—anybody who can be nice to a drunken Santa is a good guy in my book."

"You saw that?"

"It was a little hard *not* to see him. That was funny."

"I just wanted to take a silly picture. Didn't realize he was coming off a weeklong bender."

"Poor guy."

"What if we saw the same guy at O'Hare?" I ask.

"Then I'd ask Santa for a sleigh ride home." Her bright blue eyes seem extra animated.

"Enjoy your Prince."

"Enjoy your first class."

I want to say more, but I don't.

I have a feeling it won't be the last conversation I have with this dancing accountant named Cara.

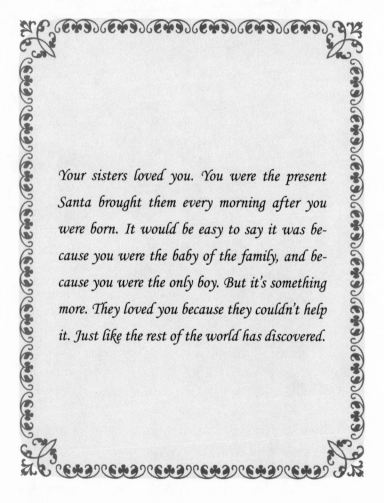

Your sisters loved you. You were the present Santa brought them every morning after you were born. It would be easy to say it was because you were the baby of the family, and because you were the only boy. But it's something more. They loved you because they couldn't help it. Just like the rest of the world has discovered.

CHAPTER FIVE

White Christmas

*W*hen I reach Liz Holdcomb's voice mail and start talking, it dawns on me where she happens to be.

"Liz, it's Heath. I'm thinking you're somewhere in Europe right now on your honeymoon. So probably you'll get this after Christmas or even after New Year's. I'm stuck at O'Hare Airport—go ahead, tell me you told me so. This is what happens when I try to book flying myself. The day before Christmas."

I pause for a moment, a hundred thoughts going through my mind.

"I hope you two lovebirds are loving life and loving each other. You deserve it. Merry Christmas. If I'm never heard from again, start looking in the Midwest. Love ya."

Liz has been my personal assistant for over a decade. I was fortunate to hire her right as my first single broke. She was trustworthy and great with people and laughed at my jokes.

There was never any sexual chemistry with Liz. I found her to be more of a sister type, and she probably thought of me as a nightlong binge away from prison. We connected and it just happened.

I've come to rely on her as more than an assistant over the years. She handles the little details of my life so I can focus on the bigger things. It's not just doing dry cleaning (which I still do, thank you very much). It's stuff like figuring out what happened to my iPad when it won't turn on. Or arranging my schedule so that I can surprise a sick girl in the hospital with a visit. Or even helping me find a counselor that I could recommend to my then-girlfriend, who needed a lot more than just counseling.

Liz got married a week ago. When she told me she had big news, I knew she was going to quit. I just knew it. Then she told me they wanted to go to Paris for their honeymoon and she needed a few weeks off. I was so relieved I almost tackled her. I told her to go, take some time off from the Heath Sawyer world. The tour was exhausting, and she could have been one of the casualties if she didn't go. Then I asked her whether she was coming back. She said she would, after Christmas.

This was all fine and dandy in theory, but it sucks at eight o'clock at night on December 23 when my flight has finally been canceled. People in the lounge have been saying this was going to happen, but I didn't pay much attention while I watched ESPN at the bar and chatted with several business-people who are stuck like me. Those men and women know how to handle situations like this. Without Liz to troubleshoot my travel plans, I'm like a third grader wondering how I'm going to get back home to Mommy.

The airport lounge has a beautifully adorned Christmas tree right at the front desk. I hear a jazzy version of "We Three Kings" playing in the background as I go ask an attendant about the delays.

"So do you know when flights will be rescheduled?"

"You'll have to check with the airlines in the morning."

"So do you give out vouchers or coupons or something like that?"

I'm thinking maybe one of those coupon books. Maybe I'll get a complimentary stay at a hotel along with another coupon for a case of beer and some buffalo wings. Of course, I don't need to worry about spending a few bucks on a hotel or a bad meal, but Momma brought me up right. Some habits are hard to break.

The gray-haired attendant, who resembles a ruler, seems to glare at me as if I'm some redneck hillbilly. Yeah, maybe I sorta am, but that doesn't mean I'm clueless and uncultured. It's the culture of celebrity that's made me clueless about taking care of myself. I have people doing everything. Or, I should say, I have Liz doing everything. And now Liz is finally living first class in one of the most romantic places in the world while I'm in the Windy City.

"We can't do anything about weather delays."

He might as well be the Soup Nazi's brother, since his stare seems to yell "NEXT!" with fury.

I nod and smile, then walk away. I wander out of the lounge, knowing I'll have to figure out a hotel to stay at. Then I can drink the night away and wait for the storm to subside, and finally get home tomorrow. Colorful Christmas lights make a halo over my head as I stroll to exit the terminal. I have a cap on and don't make eye contact with anybody. I'm in no mood for chitchat now.

That is, until I see Cara standing at a gate talking on the phone.

I realize maybe she can help. Maybe she can hold my hand again, even if she has no idea who I happen to be. Maybe it's better she doesn't know.

"Cara."

"Oh, hey."

I know I startled her by coming out of the corner behind her right after she got off the phone. "Sorry. I didn't want to interrupt you talking."

"My family is crazy."

"I wasn't eavesdropping," I tell her.

"I was explaining to my mother about being home late. She's freaking out and they're trying to figure out— I'm the person who ends up coordinating everything, so, yeah—"

She looks drained and a bit helpless as she talks. Not in a worried, frenzied sort of way, but in a truly troubled way. I want to ask her if she's okay, like, really okay, but I hate when people do that to me.

"Did you get a hotel?"

"I figured I could just tag along with you."

Those brilliant eyes suddenly look full of terror.

"No, I mean—I'm not asking if I can share a room with you."

She shakes her head, laughs, and says, "Of course not."

"That'd be strange, right?"

Suddenly I realize this is yet again the wrong thing to say.

"Yes, Heaven forbid you should shack up with me for the night. Guys really try to avoid that as much as possible."

"No, you know what I mean—"

"Not really."

I pause for a moment, trying to figure out what she's talking about. "Were you able to find a hotel?"

"It took half a dozen tries."

"What? They're all booked?"

Cara gives me an ominous nod. Next she'll bust out into a "muaaaahhahahaaha!!"

"So what'd you find?"

"An older hotel."

She doesn't say anything more. "So, are you averse to me trying to stay there too?"

"No, it's—it's the Charleton downtown. One of the oldest in the city. A producer friend of mine in Tulsa told me about it. They're not close, but they have rooms. Well, they did about two hours ago."

I'm already looking up the info on it.

"So it's not, like, a stalker thing to do to stay there myself?" I ask.

"Yes, I'm very worried." She sounds like she's back to herself now. At least, the Cara I've known for the past day.

"You might be if they say they're all booked." I'm on hold, waiting for someone to take my information. "I'm just kiddin'."

After a few minutes of talking with someone, and Cara waiting as if she actually happens to be my personal assistant, I tell her they have rooms.

"So this place isn't a dump, is it?"

"It's a hole," Cara says. "They book rooms by the hour."

"Oh, man." I shake my head. "That's fifty minutes of wasted time."

She gives a cute and polite laugh that makes me amused. I finish booking a room; then I add something since Cara is listening.

"Do you have, like, a honeymoon suite available? Something with a heart-shaped bed and mirrors on the ceiling?"

The guy on the other end of the phone simply says no. Not an amused no or a festive Christmas no but just an *I have things to do* no.

I slip my phone back in my pocket.

"You sure you don't think I'm following you or something?" I ask Cara.

"No—I know you're following me."

"Yeah, but not in any kind of creepy way."

"Well, I don't know that just yet. But you look harmless enough. Or, well—only partially harmless."

"If you only knew," I say as we start walking.

"I'm resourceful. I can handle pretty much anything."

I don't want to tell her what I'm thinking, but maybe she already can tell. Maybe she already knows I'm not exactly resourceful and have had others handle stuff for me for quite some time.

"Do you like eggnog?" she asks.

"Only the spiked kind."

"Well, I'm gonna have some when we get to the hotel. I'll let you spike your own."

"You can be my designated driver."

"Welcome to my world," Cara says.

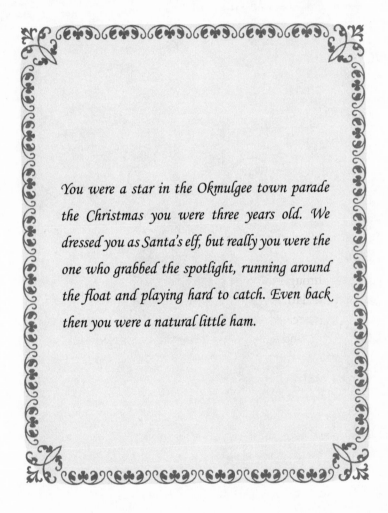

You were a star in the Okmulgee town parade the Christmas you were three years old. We dressed you as Santa's elf, but really you were the one who grabbed the spotlight, running around the float and playing hard to catch. Even back then you were a natural little ham.

CHAPTER SIX

Cold December

*T*he city of Chicago looks like a Christmas tree, with lights shining through mounds of snow and everything twinkling against the dark night sky. Michigan Avenue is lined with frozen white wreaths waving on lampposts. The last few times I've been around here, I haven't been able to look out and enjoy the sights. So many times I get off a tour bus and head into a venue and then have to leave the next day (or even the same night). The last two concerts I had around Chicago weren't even downtown but in surrounding suburbs. Life on the road looks glamorous until you're on the road in a tour bus surrounded by the same people. For weeks and months that feel like decades.

"You ever been to Chicago?" I ask Cara.

"Just a couple of times. I know I seem like the total jet-setter, but I'm really just a homebody. What about you?"

"I get to the city every now and then. Don't get to enjoy it as much as I'd like."

We're in the backseat of a cab heading to the hotel. The roads are paved, but the snow is coming down fast. And it looks thick.

"So what do you for a living? Do you come here for work?"

I look at her and see earnest wide eyes staring back at me.

"I work in securities," I say.

"You do?"

I laugh. "Nah, I just like saying that. I don't even really know what that means."

"You don't look like a financial guy."

"What do I look like?"

"Ooh, that's a hard question. The jeans and T-shirt make me think—maybe you have something to do with college kids? I don't know. Maybe a youth pastor."

The buzz in my head from the drinks at O'Hare isn't strong enough to take this comment. "Are you kiddin' me?"

"I know that's wrong. I don't know. You own your own business?"

"You could say that."

"A restaurant? A chain of them?"

"No, but I've been talking about opening one. It's gotta have a lot of meat there. I might just call it Meat Restaurant."

"Are you a farmer?" Cara asks.

"Do I look like a farmer?"

"No, no. Well, maybe. I don't know."

She fidgets in her seat. This woman is funny to watch. She's a lot of nervous energy, and even when she's quiet I can tell there's a lot going on in her brain.

"You're pretty brave traveling with someone you have absolutely no idea about," I say.

"You like meat and country music. Oh, and beer."

"I'm an all-American man."

"You don't look like an athlete."

"Hey. I'm six foot three, thank you very much. I played some football in my time."

If, of course, my time meant sometime between fourth and fifth grades.

"Sorry. Not that you're out of shape."

"I look that bad, huh?"

"No, just— I've been around athletes. I can tell."

"Too much meat and beer," I say, looking out the window and laughing. "Story of my life."

I'm trying to keep things light and cordial and non-creepy. Maybe I should be the one worried. Maybe she's a serial killer posing as a cute blue-eyed accountant. Maybe she's going to slit my throat before we get to the hotel. Maybe this isn't some funny little Christmas story I'll tell one day but rather a *Twilight Zone* episode—or worse, something out of a horror novel.

"You know, you don't exactly look like an accountant," I say. "Should I be worried?"

"So what do I look like?"

"A grade-school teacher."

She flips her hair back as she looks at me. "You wouldn't say that if you saw my grade-school teachers."

"Initially when I saw you, I would've thought someone in business. Maybe a publicist or something like that. But now with that sweater on . . ."

"*This* is keeping me warm, thank you very much." She

glances out the window and I notice her profile. Her cute little nose with a few freckles and her pink lips, parting just slightly. "It's a pretty city, isn't it?"

It is quite pretty, especially from my view.

"What if we're snowed in here?" I ask her.

"We can't be. There's just no way."

"You have to get home."

"Yes, I do."

There's an urgency in her voice that is foreign to me. "So tell me why."

"My family is counting on me."

"Mine's gonna make me feel guilty if I don't come home. Heck, they've already been making me feel guilty."

"Don't you want to go home?"

"Yes. Yes and no."

"Why the no?"

I feel my phone vibrate, but ignore it for now. "Part of me—if I'm really wanting to be honest—wants to just sit on some warm beach and drink drinks with umbrellas in them and feel the sun on my head. And just—do—nothing."

"And here I was thinking you were going to say something like stay in New York and help out all the homeless families in dire need."

"That was second on my wish list," I say, cracking up. "Man, you're tough."

"I was just keeping with that 'really wanting to be honest' part."

"See—our first night together and we're already starting to derail."

She doesn't say anything, so maybe my humor has gone unnoticed.

"I was trying to be funny."

"It works about a third of the time," Cara says.

"You're funny in your own little way, you know?"

"I'm honest, and that can sometimes be my downfall. The reason I—the reason there aren't too many nights together on the town with hunky strangers."

I nod.

"Or with people like you," she adds, refusing to give me the label of "hunky."

"I like this," I say. "I really do. It's refreshing."

"What?"

"The honesty. In my world, I don't get a lot of it."

"Wait—so are you in the financial world?"

"No. It's worse. Much worse."

We arrive at the hotel and that's our cue to head inside.

After checking in, I try to keep the awkwardness to a minimum.

"Hey—look—again, not trying to be creepy, but I'll be at the bar in another hour or so. In case you have time to kill and want men to mock."

She tightens her lips and smiles. Not flirtatious or even an into-me look. I don't know. This woman might not even be interested in guys. Not that I'm the world's best-looking guy, but I usually do better than this. This is just bizarre.

"Maybe. We'll just have to see."

I feel like a college kid, helpless and talking to a girl I know I'm never going to see again.

"Thanks for the suggestion for the hotel."

"Of course."

"And if I don't see you—maybe I'll run into you in Oklahoma."

"I'll look for you in the meat aisles where I shop."

"Or the liquor aisles. I frequent both."

She nods as if she slightly dislikes the jokes. Sorta with her nose slightly up in the air. As if I'm just slightly something. Slightly not her type. Slightly enough to make her stay in her room the rest of the night with the locks on and the DO NOT DISTURB sign on the door.

That's cool. I don't want to be disturbed either. If Cara came and sat by me, odds would be a lot greater that nobody would interrupt. They'd think I was on a date and not want to interfere. Otherwise I'm Heath Sawyer sitting in a bar begging someone to come up to my table and make idle chitchat.

We head to the elevator and the doors close.

"What floor are you on? Or do you want to keep it a secret?"

"Five."

I push five, then push ten for my room.

We ride in silence for a couple of moments. I gotta admit—I don't know what to say. I've said enough probably. I should just take my cue and shut up.

"Well, Heath, it's been a pleasure."

She shakes my hand.

Yeah, she's not showing up at the bar anytime soon.

"Safe travels. Hope you get home soon."

"Hope you do, too," Cara says, then bolts out of the elevator, wheeling her suitcase behind her.

This has been fun, talking to a stranger who has no idea who I am, and what being me usually entails. She could simply talk to a guy she doesn't know. And I could know that whatever happened and whatever she thought of me, it would be because of *me* and not because of "Heath Sawyer." We could just be a guy and a girl from Oklahoma both trying to get back home.

After all, that's still just who we all are at the end of the day. No matter how far we go or how much we think we might have changed. We all need to go back home every now and then to be reminded of where we've come from. To remember the boy or girl we once were.

Blah blah blah, Heath. Time to get drunk.

Ho ho ho. Let it snow, snow, snow.

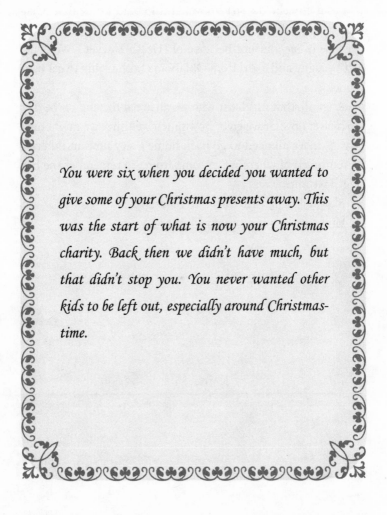

You were six when you decided you wanted to give some of your Christmas presents away. This was the start of what is now your Christmas charity. Back then we didn't have much, but that didn't stop you. You never wanted other kids to be left out, especially around Christmas-time.

CHAPTER SEVEN

2000 Miles

'm watching "Christmas in Hollis" by Run DMC on YouTube and thinking this is the sort of Christmas album I want to do. Sure, this is, like, twenty-five years old, and it's old-school rap, but hey, why should that stop me? Does the world really need my rendition of "Silver Bells"? My answer to my manager is no. His answer, of course, is that a Christmas album has to have that.

I send him a reply and a link on e-mail but figure Sam's like the rest of the world today, busy with family and shopping and friends. I don't tell him I'm stuck. He won't care, 'cause it's not interfering with a concert or something related to the business. He's all business, and that's why I pay him. To be all about business when the rest of the world starts to forget. The business will remind people. "Oh, yeah, Heath Sawyer." 'Cause if you don't remind them, they forget. Soon you'll be singing at a retirement party held at an all-you-can-eat buffet in a casino.

Not that there's anything wrong with that. Except I've done that already and I can't go back. I won't. As Sam used to tell me when I played some of the scummiest little joints, "Don't be knockin' 'cause the place might be rockin'." He used to say this before I'd take the stage, playing for five people and a drugged-out bartender. A tiny club called Flesh and Bone, where all I'd get was free beer.

I've come a long way since Flesh and Bone. I have a lot to be thankful for.

Oh, but you forget every day, don't you, big-time honky-tonk guitar man?

I hate my inner voice. It always sounds so dang off-key.

I decide to call Momma to let her know I'm spending December 23 in Chi-town. I get one of my sisters instead.

"And where are you, Heath Sawyer?"

If I'm ever too big for my britches, I'll let one of the princesses set me straight. I call them the princesses simply because that's what my sisters are. Then I joke that I'm the king and they're under my rule. (That joke never goes well, so I keep telling it over and over again.)

"Bali," I say to my middle sister, Becky. "And let me tell you—flights to Indonesia take a *long* time."

"Shut up. Where are you?"

"Chicago."

"Are you stuck?"

"What do you think?"

"So why didn't you leave earlier?"

My middle sister is a year from turning forty and she's been that old since she was eight.

"I don't know. It could be something like performing for twenty thousand people at Madison Square Garden. Oh, and not being able to control *the weather.*"

"Yeah, yeah. You always have an excuse. We told you how this Christmas was gonna be."

"Merry Christmas to you too. Here's your gift bag of shame and guilt."

"Oh, shush," Becky says. "You know Mom won't say a word and your other sisters won't even begin to question you."

"That's 'cause they love me."

"Anne adores you and Karen thinks you're funny."

"And you just hate me."

Becky is busy with her three young kids and is the most practical of the three Sawyer girls. She always likes getting to the point.

"What's Momma up to?" I ask.

"She's making the pies."

"Tell her I reserve a whole pecan pie for myself."

Becky pauses for a moment. "You think you'll be home by Christmas?"

"Sounds like a line from a song."

"Sounds like you're stalling."

"Seriously, I don't know," I tell her. "It's not looking good."

"I know. We were watching the Weather Channel talking about it."

"I will ride Frosty like a bull if that's the only way I'm getting home," I tell her. "And if he keels over in the winter blizzard, I'll do a Han-Solo-sleeping-in-the-tauntaun thing to stay alive."

"What are you talking about?"

Becky never did like sci-fi movies. Eventually she gives the phone to Momma.

"I can smell them from here," I tell her about the pies she said she'd just put in the oven.

"Where is 'here'?"

"About seven or eight hundred miles from you guys," I say. "The Windy City, which happens to be pretty windy right around now."

"You think you'll be there for long?"

"I'll make it home, Momma. I promise."

"What if the flights are canceled?"

"Don't worry. I promise. I keep my promises. Especially when I make them to you."

"We'll be praying you make it safe. The grandkids can't wait to see you."

I can't help the sigh that escapes my mouth. "Yeah, I can't wait to see all of you."

It's been so long. Way too long.

I don't want Momma to worry and I don't want her sad. So I spend the next few moments telling some jokes and making her laugh. Now that Dad is gone, she doesn't laugh the way she used to. But I'm always there for some comic relief. That's been my role. Well, it used to be. Until the singing thing sometimes got in the way. But humor is still a top priority in the Sawyer household.

"I love you," I tell Momma. "Tell everybody I'll be there soon. I'll let you know tomorrow what the forecast looks like and whether or not I'll have to buy a snowplow."

"Stay out of trouble."

"Never," I tell her before getting off the phone.

Knowing they're all there and I'm here only makes me feel more guilty than usual. And I hate guilt.

I need a drink. Fast.

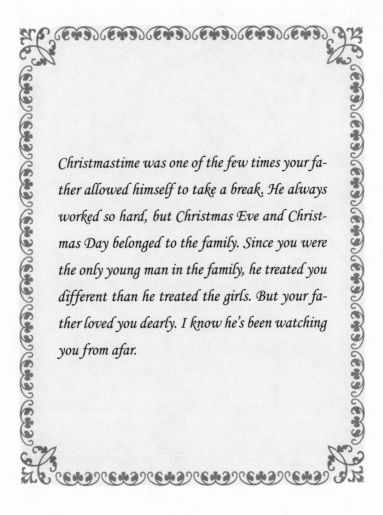

Christmastime was one of the few times your father allowed himself to take a break. He always worked so hard, but Christmas Eve and Christmas Day belonged to the family. Since you were the only young man in the family, he treated you different than he treated the girls. But your father loved you dearly. I know he's been watching you from afar.

CHAPTER EIGHT

Jingle Bell Rock

I read that this hotel was built in 1925. Narrow hallways and the ornate architecture make it appear that way. The hexagon-patterned carpet leading from the elevator to the rooms reminds me a bit of *The Shining*. The lounge is a dimly lit round room with an oval bar made of dark wood. A piano sleeps in the corner while a group is lined up, drinking and laughing. When I arrive I recognize a couple of people from the flight.

I order a rum and Diet Coke, then take it to a table in the shadows of the middle of the room. I can still see the television screens while staying out of the group party that's forming. ESPN shows highlights, while the Weather Channel shows chaos.

For a few moments, I try to see exactly what's happening with the snowstorm. All I can pick up is that the snow is going to keep coming, it's going to snow a lot, and a lot of people are going to be stranded. Especially Nashville residents stuck in Chicago heading toward Tulsa (at least, that's what I'm interpreting myself).

Stuck in an old hotel. 50% chance I see Jack Nicholson roaming halls with an ax tonight. Redrum & Rum.

An hour and several drinks later, I hear a shuffling beside my table.

"Drinking alone, huh?"

I almost don't recognize the attractive woman standing next to me. It's Cara, who has changed out of her Christmas sweater and looks a little more hip in her jeans and leather coat with a V-neck T-shirt underneath.

"Going out for a night on the town?" I ask.

"This is as exciting as it gets for me."

"That makes me feel extra special."

"You know what I mean."

"Unless you have a hot date, go ahead and take a seat," I tell her. "Can I get you anything?"

"No, thanks."

"Oh, come on."

"I'm not much of a drinker. My family does it enough for me."

I give her an understanding nod. Her hair is a little more stylized and she looks more made up than when I last saw her. Not that I was carefully studying her or anything. But I'm starting to notice a little more each time I see her.

"Want some coffee? Tea? Milk?"

I eventually get her to order a Diet Coke, which I get for her. Her eyes wander around the room, even though nobody is bothering us.

"Did you check on flights?"

I shake my head. "I wasn't in the mood to wait half an hour to hear that they don't know anything yet."

"It's supposed to be snowing here all night and all day tomorrow."

"Fabulous."

"No, it's not fabulous," she says. "Don't jinx us."

"By the time this is over, you're going to be doing shots," I joke.

My cell phone, sitting on the table, lights up, and I instinctively grab it and then squint to actually see who the text is from.

"You really need glasses," Cara says.

"It's just dark in here."

"Or maybe your eyes are telling you they're tired of you squinting."

"Never," I say.

But I'm sure Cara's right. She's probably right a lot of the time.

The text is from someone at my record label.

> Any thoughts on those demos?

I put the phone back down and ignore the question. For a while, Cara and I talk about glasses and my resistance to getting them, which is really just my resistance to getting older. And about those little gray hairs I've been seeing sprouting in my beard and my sideburns? I'm planning on fighting them all the way.

"Excuse me—Mr. Sawyer?"

I didn't even see the two young women standing beside our table.

Here it goes. This is going to be amusing.

"Can we get a picture with you?" the brunette asks.

The girls look like they might be in college or just out. I glance at Cara and see her confusion.

"Of course," I say.

I give the cell phone to Cara and say, "Mind taking it?"

"Why are they taking pictures of you?" Then Cara stands and laughs. "*Heath* Sawyer?"

The girl who asked for the photo says, "We saw you in concert when you came here this fall."

"Did I remember all my lyrics?" I ask with a grin. Cara is still holding the phone in her hand, thinking.

"Uh, picture?" I prompt her.

"Heath Sawyer," Cara says again, as she takes a couple of pictures.

The young women thank me and I tell them to have a good night. Then I sit back down and can't help the smirk on my face.

"*You're* Heath Sawyer."

"I know—they Photoshop those musical videos."

"I thought you were taller."

"Ouch," I say.

"So why didn't you tell me?"

I take a sip of my drink. "I thought you didn't like country."

"I live in Tulsa. I've at least heard of country music."

"But you didn't recognize me, did you?"

Cara wipes an eye as she shakes her head. "Maybe I need that drink now."

I realize how hard she's been laughing.

"I can get you one."

"I feel like an idiot."

"Please—I make an idiot of myself about once every twenty minutes. Or maybe seconds. I thought it was cool you didn't know."

"Oh, yeah. Way 'cool.' I'm so hip. I'm surprised to find you flying back to Tulsa."

"I don't have my own plane," I say, then add, "Yet," more for amusement than anything else.

She wears a grin like someone who was just pranked. "I kept wondering—I just kept thinking you always acted like that. Like something was up and you were amused by something. I assumed it was just yourself."

"I amuse myself pretty easily."

Cara groans and I tell her to stop.

"Really, it's no big deal. Now, if I had been Prince, you would've recognized me. Of course, I'd be about two feet smaller, so then again, who knows?"

For a moment, she's studying me the way people do. It's like they think there's this aura surrounding you once you've been featured inside *People* magazine or done a duet with Carrie Underwood.

"Yep, I know—I suddenly just got a lot better-looking, didn't I?"

I crack myself up, but she only gives me a mild smile.

"Come on—I'm kidding. You look like you want to leave."

"I sorta do," she says. "I kinda want to just throw up. Wait until my friends hear about this."

"I know some guys who would've been insulted if you

didn't recognize them. Their massive egos would be hurt and their little hearts would start to shrivel."

The young ladies who just had their picture taken with me are talking to the group at the bar, and everybody's looking at us.

Uh-oh.

"I sorta like the anonymity," I say. "Drunk businessmen can be the worst. Just watch."

Cara's eyes look bright even in the murky light of the bar. She's got a really friendly smile, the kind you'd love to bring home to your momma.

Not that I'm bringing any smile or anybody home. Just a random observation.

I keep seeing smiles and conversation among the mob at the bar.

"Listen—promise me something," I say. "I'm not playing songs on that piano. Got it? Please—tell me I'm not playing songs on that piano. It ain't gonna happen."

The way she smiles tells me she wants to get back at me for not telling her. It also tells me there's something there. There's absolutely something there.

Suddenly I don't really mind if it's because of the name. I like the way she's looking at me right now.

Midway through belting out "Jingle Bell Rock" on the piano, I know I'm having way too much fun. I saw this coming and didn't really want to be behind the piano, but I couldn't help it. There's not a guitar in sight, but thankfully (or unfortunately) I know some tunes on the piano. I've got a crowd around, drinking and buying me drinks and laughing and singing along. Half of us are trapped in the city, so what else is there to do?

Cara stands near the piano, looking a little like *What have I gotten myself into?* I told her to rescue me, but instead she encouraged me to get behind the piano. Someone said to sing a Christmas song, so that's what I've been playing.

"Play 'Dusty Rooms,'" one of the women who first spotted me shouts out.

She's having a little too much fun too.

"Dusty Rooms" is one of my earliest hits and should always be played on the guitar. I grimace even as I'm still singing the Christmas tune.

"Can you do 'Lone Ranger'?" someone else asks.

"How about 'Grandma's Got a New Man'?"

"How about 'Honky Tonk Badonkadonk'?" one of the businessmen calls out.

"That's Trace Adkins," a woman tells him.

I actually try my best to play the chorus of the last song for a few seconds. The crowd hollers in laughter.

"The other titles are my songs," I tell Cara as I'm playing the chords of one of my hits.

She still looks embarrassed.

"She doesn't listen to country," I say to the crowd.

As Cara gets teased, I try to remember how to play "Grandma's Got a New Man." That's always a crowd favorite and gets everybody laughing.

"Daddy's in denial and Momma's in mourning. Grandma got a makeover. Should've been a warnin'."

The song is simple, really, but it's all about the lyrics. Half of the group sings along, especially when I get to the chorus.

"False teeth, a hearin' aid, and a fake ol' tan. Better watch out. Grandma's got a new man. There are things I just don't understand. Better watch out. Grandma's got a new man."

At one point I look over at Cara and she's wiping tears away from her eyes from laughing so hard.

Well, that's one way to get an emotion.

"Told you my songs are deep stuff," I say as I finish the song and take another drink. "I got another called 'Redneck Reject.' People love that one too."

I drain my drink. I could keep doing this all night. The buzz is always better when you have people to fly alongside.

"Play 'Man Card'!" another stranger shouts.

Cara's expression seems to say, *Who are you again and what kind of songs do you write?*

You don't need twenty thousand people to have a good time. You don't even need a guitar (though it sure helps). You just need someone to carry a tune and some fun lyrics about something silly or something everybody is already thinking.

Eventually I stand up and wave my hands.

"Anything more and I gotta start charging," I joke.

I make chitchat for a bit but then see that Cara's ready to leave. Something's changed since she learned my identity. She's got all the signs as her heels slowly start inching away toward the doors. Someone gives me a drink and I thank them. I finally manage to break away from the crowd and wish them a good night. Cara's near the exit.

"You don't have to leave," she tells me.

"Nah, it's fine. It's good."

I follow her to the elevator.

"You're quite the performer."

"Oh, I was just havin' a little fun."

"Now I'm going to download all your albums. How many do you have?"

"Eight studio albums," I say, then add, "But who's counting?"

The moment we get in the elevator, she looks quite uncomfortable. She would be a horrible poker player, because every single emotion she seems to have shows up on her face.

"Look, I, uh—this was fun. I'm just callin' it a night. I don't want any sort of awkward thing before I go."

I nod.

"What?" she asks.

"Nothing."

"What's that smirk for?"

I act shocked even though I knew I had the smirk. "You're the first girl I ever serenaded who didn't want to hang out afterwards."

"*That* was a serenade?" she asks. "Those tunes really put a girl in the mood."

"I have some that do. So I've been told."

"You have two big fans downstairs who would probably tell you that tonight."

Man, she's got a bite about her. Not sure what I've done to deserve this.

The doors open and she steps out. I stand between them to keep the doors open.

"Did I do anything to offend you?" I ask.

These words seem strange coming out of my mouth. I'm usually not so worried about offending someone. But I'm curious, especially since I might not see her again.

"Does the party ever stop for you?"

"Yeah. Usually a few days in February. I can't remember when, but I can let you know."

"Funny," Cara says, not smiling.

"I'm tryin'."

"Trying to do what?"

"I thought you were having a good time downstairs."

"It's fun watching. But the show is over, right?"

"Doesn't have to be."

The drinks I've had allow this last line to slip out. It's already so obvious. Like, painfully obvious. The way I'm looking at her and the way I'm standing, waiting and watching and wanting. All of that doesn't need a line like "Doesn't have to be."

"I think I liked you more when I didn't know who you were," Cara says.

"Ouch. Wow—I really didn't play this one well at all, did I?"

"There's nothing to play. This isn't a game and I'm not a set of dice you can pick up and roll."

"Hey, that's good."

Cara nods. "Keep it. It's yours. It's not 'Grandma's Got a New Man,' but it's something."

She starts to walk away.

"Good night," I call out. "Maybe good-bye."

"Maybe," she says turning back toward me briefly.

I swear I think she's smiling.

Picture the prettiest Christmas tree you've ever seen. You were six when you decided to put a homemade star on the top. All by yourself. An eight-foot tree when you were only half that size. I have to give you credit for trying. But I still remember hearing the crash and thinking someone had fallen to their death. The tree toppled over and every ornament seemed to fall and crack. We found you still clinging to one side, freaked-out. I still think of that and can't help but laugh.

CHAPTER NINE

Silent Night

I get off on the wrong floor.

I'm not going to blame the rum—rather, I'll blame Cara. I'll blame the fact that I know for certain she came down to see me. She changed and got a little more dressed up for me. Not that it meant I'd be going back to her hotel room. But her sudden change of mind surprises me.

Then again, most things women do surprise me.

Naomi hasn't called, and that worries me a bit. It makes me think she might be on the lookout for me. Maybe she's at this hotel now. Maybe she conned the front desk man into getting into my room (she's done that before). Maybe she's waiting to seduce me. And right now, the way I'm feeling, I kind of hope she is waiting. Kind of.

Then again, the way this trip is going, I'm going to see twin Naomis standing in front of me on this hexagon-patterned carpeting, holding hands and grinning and telling me to come play with them.

"Forever and forever . . ."

Maybe my manager, Sam Goldberg, will come riding down the hallway on a Big Wheel talking with his finger pointed at me.

I have no idea why a horror movie is going through my mind, but it's been a long day and a longer nine months. The last time I slowed down was maybe a year or two ago. It would've been nice not to be left alone in this old hotel with the creepy carpet like this. It would've been nice to get to know Cara the accountant a little better. Or a lot better.

There's a door I'm approaching that's halfway open. That's when it dawns on me that I'm on the wrong floor. I slow down and then pause to look inside the room. I spot the white boots right away. Then something red.

Those are pants.

Red and white fluffy pants. As if Santa rushed into the room and got naked and forgot to shut the door.

For a second, I wonder if this is a prank. I don't hear anything, but I see the Santa Claus pants clearly now, resting in a pile on the floor. I might have to squint to read my messages on my phone, but there's no way I can miss this.

I take out my cell phone and start to take a picture, but the door suddenly slams shut. I stand there, wondering if a naked Jolly Saint Nick is behind the peephole watching me. I wave at the door like the drunken fool I am. Then I head back down to the elevator to get to my floor.

*   *   *

I can't sleep. All I can do is think about my father.

I knew covering George Jones's "He Stopped Loving Her Today" was going to do it. I shouldn't have gone there. It's been six months and one week and three days and I've managed to not go there. But tonight of all nights, I went there. I played a song Dad taught me, one he loved, one that got me into this business.

Dad should still be here. Not in the room in the middle of Chicago, but on this earth breathing and smiling and laughing and joking and listening.

I still have so many songs I want to sing, but sometimes I wonder, What's the point if he's not gonna be around to hear them? I still have so many questions I want to ask, but lately I've been wondering what I'm going to do now that he's not there to answer them.

Momma and the girls are there, and that's a good thing because "I gotta take care of them." So I say, but really, I know it's the other way around. I know they're the ones who are gonna take care of me. Except, I'm a man and I can do fine on my own. I can take care of myself. I can keep my emotions in check and sing about wild nights and women and whiskey and I can keep from crying. Right?

So if that's the case, why are there tears on my cheeks right now?

It's late and I'm a bit bombed and I know I need to at least attempt to close my eyes and do the thing people do at three a.m. But I'm thinking of Paul Sawyer. I'm thinking of the things I should've told him before he died. I'm thinking of what Christmas is going to be without him, and how I've spent half a year running from thinking about any of this.

Stop your moping, Heath.

I love my songs because they make people smile. They bring people together to sing along and cheer and holler and have a good time. That's what I'm known for. That's what I do. That's why I hate this melancholy sort of stuff. Hate it. But, man, it still comes. It happens to the best of us, right? There's no way to control it.

Even though you've been trying to run and control it for a long time, right, Heath baby? Even though you've kept trying to write feel-good songs that keep coming out with a feel-bad vibe.

I sit in a chair and take a sip of water and scroll through my phone. It's fun when you're in front of the masses. But when you're by yourself, you gotta deal with this on your own. You can't perform to yourself.

I notice the finger that could have easily had a wedding ring on it. That ship sailed six years ago with the woman I sent away. I ran away from her memory just like I've been running from my father's passing. The pain hurts, especially when you see it in a mirror.

I want to get home and deal with the grief I've managed to sing away for half a year. The noise has vanished and the silence has crept in. I'm in another room that I can't claim as my own, feeling drained by spirits as false as their advertising and wishing someone else was here with me.

For a moment, I think of Naomi and how alone I felt as I dealt with my father's decline and passing by myself. I felt alone even though she was there. A warm body can never take the place of a caring soul.

Then I think of Cara. I think of her holding my hand on that plane ride. I haven't had a tender moment like that—a genuine, unforced moment—in a long time. It reminded me of my childhood for some reason.

I like thinking of her because she makes me smile. It's crazy to think about her, but at three in the morning it's crazy simply to be awake thinking about anything at all. At least it's something refreshing to focus on.

Every now and then everybody needs their hand held. Doesn't matter who you are or where you're heading.

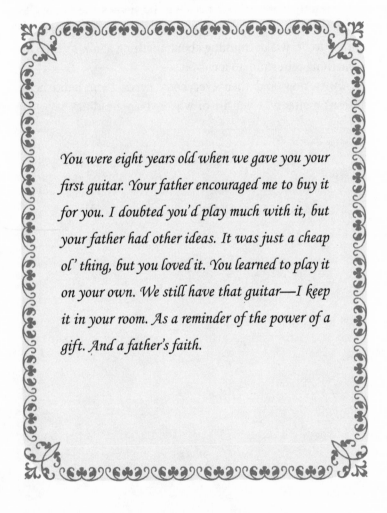

You were eight years old when we gave you your first guitar. Your father encouraged me to buy it for you. I doubted you'd play much with it, but your father had other ideas. It was just a cheap ol' thing, but you loved it. You learned to play it on your own. We still have that guitar—I keep it in your room. As a reminder of the power of a gift. And a father's faith.

CHAPTER TEN

Step into Christmas

$\mathcal{I}$ wake up and realize I slept through my alarm. Then I see that I'm still holding on to my phone. Then I see that I never quite completed the job of setting the time that I wanted to wake up this morning.

It's seven minutes after nine. If I have neighbors next to my room, they hear the angry curses I let out as I jump up and go to my computer.

My goal had been to get up around six and check on the eight o'clock flight they had booked me on. As far as I know, my flight might be up in the sky right now. As I'm trying to find the right place to check on my laptop, I listen to the voice mail someone left me early this morning.

What about Cara? Why didn't she call and try to wake me up?

I know I gave her my number, but that doesn't mean she's

suddenly responsible for me. She's not Liz. And maybe after last night, she might not ever want to use that number.

Someone from the airline is telling me the flights have been delayed and to check with them to see when they'll be re-scheduled. I'm still groggy and hungover from last night, so it's taking a minute to connect the dots. I go over to the window and open the heavy velour drapes. The world outside is white and blurry and definitely not suitable to fly in or even step out-side in.

I let out a sigh, then sit down on my bed.

It's Christmas Eve, and I'm in a room at the Charleton Hotel.

I don't want to be stuck here for another twenty-four hours. My liver and my soul might not be able to take it.

"Look, man, I'll give you a call when I figure out what's going on."

I slip out of the elevator as I head to the front desk to ask for help. I'm talking to a buddy, Jackson, who I haven't spoken to in several years. He's someone I know, a guitarist who played with me a couple of tours ago and now lives in Chicago.

"If you don't mind hanging around with a two-year-old, you can stay with us."

The thought of Jackson with a kid is terrifying.

Well, almost as terrifying as the thought of Heath Sawyer with a kid.

"Uncle Heath," I say. "Sonja would love that."

"She's always had a crush on you."

"I'd love to see you guys, honestly. I'll let you know what I find out about traveling home. I gotta get home today."

"How's your mom doing?" he asks.

"She's doing okay, considering everything. But Christmastime is gonna be hard. I promised I'd be home."

"The prodigal son returns."

"Yeah, you got that right," I tell him before saying goodbye.

I'm heading to the desk when I hear someone call my name. The voice sounds like a woman's voice, but low. Like, strange low. I peer around the lobby, waiting to see God knows what.

"Heath Sawyerrrrrrrrrr."

I spot a familiar face peering from behind a Christmas tree at the side of the lobby, and I saunter over.

"Sorry, no time for autographs," I tell her.

"Are you Brad Paisley?" Cara asks in her mock low creepy voice.

"No. I'm a lot better-looking."

"Now I know you're funny."

"So you've heard of *him*, huh?"

Cara's hair is pulled back in a ponytail. She's wearing tattered jeans with some cool military half boots and a black sweater, and her black coat with a long dotted scarf draped around her. It's a casual look but not a lazy casual, like I seem to usually have. For me, it's always the same hairstyle and always the same look. I like keeping a bit of scruff. Just to show I live on the edge. Just to show how dangerous I can really be.

Or maybe 'cause you're lazy and don't like shaving.

That too.

I see she's got her suitcase in her hand.

"Did you find a flight out of here?" I ask.

"Nope."

She looks like she's holding some information that she's dying for me to ask about, that she's been waiting to tell me.

"All flights are still canceled?" I ask.

"Completely. Nothing is getting out of O'Hare anytime soon."

Cara looks amused, as if she enjoys keeping whatever it is she knows from me.

"You remind me of one of my sisters," I tell her.

"Why's that?"

"Oh, you just do."

'Cause you like to torture me.

"Well, I'm going to ask the front desk if they have any suggestions," I say.

"Okay."

"What? Come on, just tell me."

"Tell you what?"

"You have it written all over you. Come on. Did you find a way out?"

"You might say that," she says.

"Obviously, if you didn't want me to know, you wouldn't have called me over here. Since you don't like playing games. Right?"

"Did that hurt your feelings last night?"

"I'm still deeply wounded. It was hard to get out of bed this morning."

"In your state, I can see why," Cara says.

I only shake my head.

"Amtrak," she says. "When was the last time you took a train ride?"

"And they're running? In this weather?"

I hear some howling, and then two women in their late fifties interrupt us. I smile and greet them and tell them how I'm stuck in Chicago. They joke about me staying with them over the Christmas holiday.

"And is this your lady friend?" one of the women asks me.

Sometimes it amuses me that people feel they know you so well they can suddenly be so personal like this only seconds after meeting you. Cara immediately states exactly who she happens to be.

"No, no, I'm just someone stuck on a plane heading to Tulsa like he is. Or was."

Cara's whole face has turned a bright red. It's cute.

"I just can't shake her," I say, feigning a whisper to the women. "Can you call the police?"

"And here I was trying to help you get home."

"Where'd you book it? Oh, thanks, nice to meet you ladies. So where?"

"Ask the concierge."

"When does the train leave?"

"A couple of hours."

"Thanks for telling me."

"If I'd had your number, I would've called," Cara says.

I start to walk to the front desk, then pause and turn around. "I thought I gave that to you last night?"

"Your Web site isn't your phone number."

I laugh and realize I did have my share of beverages last night. "So, you asking me for my number?"

"Oh, that's right. I'm sorry. I forgot who I was talking to."

She's tough. I just shake my head and look offended. "I'm not some kind of deck of cards you can just shuffle anytime you want to."

She doesn't smile at my comment. Instead, she turns and heads toward the front doors of the hotel. I don't push my luck, especially since I'm probably not done traveling with this woman.

I already feel like I've known Cara for a long time. And I'm not sure if that's a good thing or a bad one.

Before getting a cab to the Amtrak station nearby, I get a call from my manager.

"Hey—glad I got you," Sam tells me.

This is unusual because normally I don't hear from him around the holidays.

"Did you see my e-mail that I'm stuck in Chicago?"

"What? You didn't make it home?"

"Nope. I'm taking the train now. All planes are on hold."

"The train? All the way to Oklahoma?"

"Maybe it'll inspire a song," I say.

"Look—I have some bad news. The duet isn't gonna happen."

I pause for a minute. I thought that was already a done deal. So done that I haven't been thinking or worrying about it for a while. "For real? How come?"

"They didn't say. I think it came down to the songwriting credit."

"It's my song."

"They want half."

I laugh. I mention the name of the singer I'd been working six months to collaborate with.

"I wrote that song *just* for her."

"Yeah, I know."

"Her name is *in* the song," I remind Sam.

"They won't budge."

Sam Goldberg has been my manager for years and I know his personality. At the core he's a caring guy, but he also doesn't mince words. He has a computer-like analytical nature about him. When a door shuts or a connection breaks, he simply finds another one to make. He always—always—moves on. That's probably why he's managed to stay in the business for decades.

"Man, I loved that song," I tell him.

"I did too. You'll just have to write another one."

The song I wrote for *her* was centered around the banter between me and the country princess everybody knows and loves. We joke back and forth, and the chorus is a crowd-pleaser. It would have been great to perform at the Country Music Awards.

"Maybe Santa will bring you a nice little tune tomorrow morning," Sam tells me before we trade Christmas greetings and say good-bye.

I'm not hopeful. Santa hasn't been very good to me so far.

And Christmas—and Okmulgee—seem a long way away.

You didn't want anything to do with the school Christmas play. In the same way your father thought buying you a guitar would be a good idea, I thought having you perform in front of people would be a good experience. Sure, it was A Christmas Carol and you played one of the ghosts, but the experience was still great. I could tell you loved making the crowd laugh, even at times when they shouldn't be laughing. You've never stopped doing this either.

CHAPTER ELEVEN

Run, Rudolph, Run

We've been sitting in the cold taxi for just a few minutes when I thank Cara.

"What for?"

"For waitin' on me. I appreciate it, even if you find me slightly repugnant."

"It's what I do. And obviously I don't find you repugnant."

"It's what you do? Taking care of stranded strangers?"

"More like taking care of lost souls," she says.

I nod. "Doesn't anybody ever take care of you?"

For a second, she doesn't say anything but looks down. She wasn't expecting that.

"I do fine by myself, thank you very much," she finally says.

"Yeah, I don't."

"That's why you have agents and managers."

This time I pause for a moment and think. "Sometimes you need a voice of reason. Someone you can trust."

I picture my father for a second.

"Then other times you just need a nice cold beer," I say, falling back into my well-worn persona.

Cara seems to want to say more but doesn't.

After paying the cabdriver who drove Cara and me to Chicago's Union Station, I step out and nearly get bit by a Canada goose. It's just walking around the snowy sidewalk and seemed not to like the direction I was headed. Cara passed without even seeing it, but it's sticking its long neck and its sharp beak out at me as if I offended it.

It looks at me like a Chicago Bears fan might.

You comin' toward me? Yeah, don't even think about it.

Back home I'd just shoot this bird and later serve it up on a biscuit.

The snow drifts sideways as I start walking into the station. The roads are plowed, but the snow is still coming down fast. The skies above look thick and dark. My leather coat isn't the best to wear in wintertime. My boots—well, it's rare when I'm not wearing them. My hands are freezing. Mostly I just want to get out of this city and get home.

Even though I'm wearing a Budweiser baseball cap, I'm still spotted by a couple who flank me and tell me it's their honeymoon. They take a picture of me as Cara watches from a distance. We don't get far before it happens again. I oblige the strangers, trying to be friendly, always trying not to act like I'm too important to stop and talk.

"How do you get around anywhere?" Cara eventually asks as we stand in the majestic great hall next to a couple of Christmas trees decked out to the max.

"Normally I'm not lost like this."

"You're not lost. You're just stuck."

"Hopefully not anymore," I tell her. "I'm going to be highly disappointed if the train plan doesn't work."

"I hope you know you're telling that to a total control freak and people-pleaser."

"Maybe that's why I like you," I joke.

I spot some restaurants and then wonder if there's a store around.

"What do you mean, 'a store'?"

"I need to buy some Christmas presents," I say.

"It's Christmas Eve and you still need to buy Christmas presents? For who?"

I shrug. "For everybody."

"For everybody? Heath—good heavens, what are you thinking?"

"That's the problem. I wasn't."

"For everybody? Even your mother?"

"I've been busy."

"Yeah, she was busy for nine months *carrying you in her stomach* and cooking, cleaning, and taking care of you for eighteen years. But no, you're too busy."

"You sound like one of my sisters," I tell her again. "I generally have someone do this for me, but she's been busy gettin' married."

She shakes her head. I look around, determined, but all I see is fast-food restaurants. "I don't think a McDonald's gift card will really be appreciated," I say.

"What kind of shopping were you planning on doing?"

"I like gift cards. Or cash."

"That's so impersonal."

"Hey—who doesn't love an iTunes gift card?"

Cara shakes her head, her eyes penetrating me. "No, no. You don't buy them songs. You should write them a song."

"They'd prefer cash," I say. "Especially my sisters. Forget Heath Sawyer songs."

That gets a smile out of her. She can look so tough one moment, but the smile makes everything about her change.

And why exactly are you thinking this anyway, Heath?

"You're not going to find them anything here. Maybe when we get to Kansas City."

"I still think cash is going to work the best."

"That's so thoughtful. Here's a wad of cash. I slipped it in a Big Mac wrapper. Merry Christmas."

"Good idea. Forget the Christmas paper."

I see her golden ponytail shaking back and forth. "Are all men the same?"

"Yep," I say. "Even the ones who lie and say they aren't."

I recognize crazy when I see it, and she's approaching me right now.

I think if you spend enough time in the spotlight, you see a siren warning walking toward you. Maybe 'cause you've seen enough of them. Maybe 'cause of the way the eyes zone in on you like a zombie ready to sink its teeth in your neck.

"Heath Sawyer!"

The awe and the voice and the volume. This one might be trouble.

I just nod and don't stand up. I see others looking my way, but I've been left alone with my smartphone up to now.

"Is that really you?" Her voice and her expression are flat like a robot's. Yet she seems to be excited that she has spotted me.

"No," I say, trying to joke but not really joking. "Absolutely not. I'm his stunt double."

"What are you doing in Chicago?"

"Tryin' to get home."

The woman is probably forty, and she's not exactly ugly or homely or anything like that. It's that look. A cuckoo-for-Cocoa-Puffs sort of look. The kind of look that somebody who knocks on your hotel room door at midnight has. Even after you've told them no thanks. Even after you've specifically asked them to leave you alone.

"Are you taking the train?" she says in an autobot way.

Her mouth stays open, as if she's an opera singer. It's kinda funny.

"This is the airport, right?" I look around, feigning surprise.

Her head scrunches into her shoulders and then she giggles in such a scary way that I almost crouch back down in my seat.

"You're so funny."

"Thanks."

When you're famous, your jokes don't have to be funny to get a laugh.

She seems to spot Cara for the first time. That's the thing with ladies like this. They suddenly don't see anyone or anything. She smiles and gives a nervous nod.

"Nice to meet you," I say, hoping she will get the point. She doesn't.

"We used your song in our wedding," the woman says.

"Isn't that sweet?" Cara asks. "Which one was that?"

"'Redneck Reject.'"

Cara's smile fades a bit. I grin.

Of course you used that song. That explains everything.

"I'm Molly Candellbray. Not CandelaB-R-A but B-R-A-Y."

"That—is—awesome," I say. "I have to— Excuse me."

I need to get run over by a plane. Oh, wait. They're not flying.

Instead I go to the restroom. To hide. For an hour or so.

When I see myself in the mirror a few minutes later, I realize how unhealthy I look. I've lost some weight on the tour, and my plaid shirt doesn't fit as well as it used to. I'm pale, and those eyes everybody always comments on simply look tired, with carry-on luggage underneath them. I feel like I've aged five years since starting the tour.

I realize I really don't want to go home. I should want to, but it's sorta like buying a Christmas present. I should want to go shopping and find my mother and my sisters Christmas presents. I used to be that way, but then suddenly things changed. Suddenly it felt like all I was doing was being about the business of Heath Sawyer.

Sometimes I'd like to leave the business behind.

But I'm busy checking e-mail and busy being me. Busy working my life away when I need to start living a little of it again.

Moments later, I see the coast is clear next to Cara.

"Where'd she go?"

"She'll be back," Cara says with a smile.

"That's not funny."

"She's heading to Kansas City. And she's an über fan. She knows *every single song by heart.*"

Cara then makes a face as if she's trying to imitate the stranger we just met.

"You're seriously just like one of my sisters," I tell her.

"You keep saying that."

"'Cause you keep actin' like it."

"You see—the bad thing is that I've heard this before. From other guys. Now you know why I'm traveling by myself on Christmas."

"So, wait—you're traveling by yourself? What am I?"

"Oh, we're traveling together?" she asks.

"I'm sorta just tagging along since I'm a bit helpless."

"You really are, aren't you?"

"I hate details," I tell her.

"Like getting Christmas presents for Christmas Day."

"Exactly."

For a second, I look at her with her stylish jeans and boots and whole getup. Underneath the sweet look and the strong attitude, there's something very appealing. I just don't buy her line that guys tell her she's like one of their sisters.

"I bet you have a lot of guys chasing you and you're just sayin' all that."

"You have to go out of the house to find boys to chase after you," she says. "That's my problem. Well, one problem anyway."

I see the Lady in Awe coming our way again.

"I gotta leave again."

"You can run but you can't hide," Cara calls out after me.

You always liked to make everybody laugh. Remember those times when you'd be cracking jokes and your sisters and me would be crying from laughter? I knew you'd use that humor at some point in your life. I thought maybe in sales or in stand-up comedy. Little did I know you'd do a little bit of both, except you'd do them with a guitar in your hands.

CHAPTER TWELVE

Santa Claus Is Comin' to Town

"So do you want to get together and grab a drink or something on the train?" I ask Cara as we stand near the waiting Amtrak train car.

"Oh, sure, that's exactly what you want," she says in her nervous, energetic way.

"I wouldn't ask if I didn't want to."

"I don't know. Do they even serve alcohol on here?"

"I have some little bottles in case of emergencies."

Cara nods. "I bet you do. You know—I'm good."

"That's the first thing you ever said to me."

"That's right."

I smile and nod. "Well, I'm sure I'll see you when we get to Kansas City. Or beforehand."

"You never know."

"No, you don't."

For a minute she pauses, and I'm not sure what else to say or do. There's nothing left to do, right? Hugging would be odd, and shaking her hand so official.

"All right, then, see you there," she says.

Cara heads off to the car with regular seats while I go find the one with the sleeper cars. I have a small roomette that has a couple of seats facing each other next to a window. It's on the second story and the view (according to the woman at the hotel) is nicer, but come to think of it, there's not much of anything to view between here and Oklahoma. I'll be able to view the livestock and the farmlands more carefully.

If they don't serve liquor in my car, I'm going to serve some to myself. I have about a dozen little bottles of everything. My own personal to-go stash.

I'm situated and the seat is actually really roomy and comfortable. When we finally start moving, I call home.

I didn't want to call without some good news.

Momma answers. Thankfully.

"I'm on my way."

"Did you get a flight?" she asks me in her soft little voice.

"Well, sorta. I'm taking the train."

"The train?"

"When was the last time you took the train?"

"Your father liked to take the train to save money," she says. "Years ago when I'd still travel."

"I have my own little room," I tell her. "Sleeps two people. I might fall asleep and wake up in Los Angeles."

"Well, don't do that."

Momma is so cute at times because she doesn't always get my sense of humor. My sarcasm. Sometimes I tell her I'm just messin' around, but other times I don't want to be mean. That's just Momma being Momma.

"Maybe I'll have to get you to come on one of these trains with me," I tell her.

"Maybe."

"How is everyone?"

"Wonderin' when you're comin' home."

"I know—I can just picture the girls standing by the windows, waiting in anticipation."

Momma laughs at that one. Even she knows that's a ridiculous thought. My sisters won't wait around for anybody. They're always doing something, always on the go, and if not, they're in the kitchen together talking and laughing and making fun of me.

"We're cooking a ham for dinner."

"Save some of it."

"We're having turkey tomorrow."

"I'm hungry. I've had nine months of bad food."

"Then you come on home," she says.

"How's the weather by you?"

"It's fine. Just a blizzard."

She cracks me up. "Oh, 'just a blizzard.'"

"Do you have a ride from the train station?"

"Aren't you comin' to pick me up?"

"I can," Momma says.

"I'm kiddin'. Let me call you when I get there. I still don't know. I've never ridden a train before. Or at least not Amtrak. I don't know if they get delayed or not."

"You can't have Christmas dinner on a train."

"Heaven forbid."

"All by yourself."

"I've found a friend. She's travelin' to Tulsa."

"Oh, no."

"What?"

"Is she another one of those women you seem to like to bring home?"

"Momma," I say in mock shock. "You make them sound like professionals I just hired for the night."

"What about that Holly girl?"

That was indeed a mistake that I don't think my family will ever let me live down.

"This woman isn't like Holly. You'd like her."

"Is she from Tulsa?"

"Yeah, in a roundabout way, I believe."

"I don't like those L.A. girls."

Momma will always be Momma, no matter what happens.

I'm about to go—I almost do my regular routine of saying I have to go—but this time I don't because I don't have to go.

"How are you doing?" I ask her.

"I just put in a load of darks," she says.

"No. Not *what* you're doing but *how* are you doing?"

"I'm fine."

"Really?"

"I'm as fine as is to be expected."

I wait for more, but more doesn't come. I know that even if Momma was sitting there heartbroken and distraught, she'd never let on. Especially not with me.

"Don't let the girls work you too hard," I say.

"It's those wild children that have me runnin'."

"I'll call you soon. Hopefully."

"I'm prayin' for you."

"Yeah," I tell her. "Story of my life."

When I hang up, I see that Naomi called. I'd rather be punched in the face than talk to her now. I ignore the call and the subsequent text. I mix some rum with Sprite and then find my headphones. I start to listen to Christmas music, but I get bored and start exploring other songs. I think about listening to more of the demos they've sent me, but that's gonna put me back in business mode. I want to listen to music just for the enjoyment and the connection. Soon I'm daydreaming and drifting off to the sounds of other musicians and other bands that I love.

When I was a kid, I'd lose myself in music. Listening to it and then soon trying to play it. I was an ordinary kid who loved to be outdoors and loved to get into trouble, but somehow once I discovered music, that was it. That's what I wanted to do. I wanted to be one of the Georges. George Jones. George Strait. I wanted to tell stories and rock and roll and have some fun.

I finish my drink and realize fun has been hard to come by lately. Not the "fun" that I've probably taken for granted, but the fun in the little things. The minor miracles and the small victories. Now it's not even about having a number one hit. It's about sustaining that for several weeks, and following up with another hit, and making the album a hit. It's like I'm Rocky just slugging away at the poor slab of beef there in the cooler. Except, I'm not Rocky in the first movie. I'm more like Rocky III. And that's a scary thought.

My appreciation for things outside the country world has grown. I find a track from a unique singer named James Blake.

Then the volume cranks up with something from the last Thirty Seconds to Mars album, one of those raise-the-roof crowd-pleasers. Then some new country comes on with the cute couple Thompson Square singing back and forth with each other.

The love for the music is still there. The business of making it sometimes can be draining, but the music always gives a little back. Every time I listen to a good song, it gets me motivated to write again.

I'm almost asleep when there's a knock on the door.

Couldn't wait, huh?

I smile and stand up to open it.

The Lady in Awe is standing in my doorway. Unfortunately, I'm not holding a can of Mace.

"It's Molly Candellbray, remember?"

Oh, yeah, I remember.

I'm in big trouble here.

You were twelve years old when you surprised all of us with unique Christmas presents. And calling them "unique" is being kind. You had found a used book with a picture of a beautiful woman on the cover and told me it reminded you of me. The only problem was that this was one of those trashy romance novels. I enjoyed it until your father took it away. Thankfully you chose to give this to me instead of to your teenage sisters.

CHAPTER THIRTEEN

Carol of the Bells

"*T*here you are!"

I smile at Cara, who is sitting in the lounge car of the train. She stands up as I turn around for a second to see if Crazy Lady is watching me. Then I engulf Cara in my arms and feel her body suddenly grow rigid.

"Honey, I was wondering where you went," I tell her.

Molly Candellbray spent ten minutes by my doorway until I told her I needed to check on my girlfriend. Molly, of course, didn't seem fazed and just waited where she stood, so I decided to go find Cara myself. Thankfully she's sitting in here as if waiting on me.

Cara blushes and is about to say something when I open my mouth and roll my eyes upward to try to let her know who is watching us. At first she pulls back, as if she's afraid I'm going to kiss her. Then she looks around my shoulder, sees Molly, and gets it.

"Well, I've been looking for you, too, you little marshmallow."

I give her a quizzical look and she realizes that made little sense.

"So I just wanted to make sure you didn't get lost on the train," I tell her, then mouth the words, *Please, God, help me now.*

"Okay, honeybottoms."

Wow, she's really bad at this.

"So I'll see you in just a few minutes, right?" I ask her, nodding, begging.

"Sure," she says slowly. "See you. With all my stuff, right?"

I nod. "Yes, honey. Honey*bottoms.* I'm gonna go back in now. See you soon."

As I start to walk back to the door of the lounge car, I just smile at Molly. She's watching me with suspicious eyes. Or maybe that's just the look she was born with. The kind of mad boil-the-rabbit sort of eyes that make men smile and start sprinting the other way. The kind that keep following me back into my own train car.

"So that's your girlfriend?" Molly asks in a loud whisper after the door between the cars closes behind us.

"Yes," I shout back in a mock whisper. "So don't tell anybody."

"What happened to the other woman? She was so attractive."

Something in me wants to stick up for Cara, even though she can't even hear this conversation. "I decided to replace her with something more beautiful."

I get back in my roomette and don't plan on opening the sliding glass door again unless I know for sure it's Cara. I pull the privacy curtain closed so that I'll be left alone, protected from Fan Girl 666.

We're moving through murky, snow-covered farmlands when the knock comes.

"Yes?"

"It's Cara."

"Are you sure?" I ask as I pull back the curtain. "Name one of my songs."

"'Friends in Low Places'?"

I laugh and open the door. "Ah, I knew it was you. Hurry before Misery comes."

"Misery?"

"That's what I'm calling her. Her name is Molly, but I'm getting the *Misery* vibe. You know—the movie."

"Never saw that."

"So you don't know movies either?" I ask her as the door shuts.

"I do. Hey, nice room. Tight but nice."

I point at the chair that faces the one I was sitting in. "A seat just for you."

"A lot better view than where I was sitting," she says as she looks out the window. I put her bag in the small spot next to the wall.

"It's looked that way for the whole ride. Foggy fields and cloudy skies and cows mooning me."

"So did that woman just sneak in here?"

"No—it's just I'm not so good at sending fans away. I've had some problems before where I've said something or done something and the next thing I know, I'm reading about it on-line somewhere."

"Do you, like, physically assault these people or some-thing?"

"Of course not," I say. "But some really get their feelings hurt. Especially if I say they're a freak or something."

"Well, yeah. Maybe don't use words like *freak*. Just a sug-gestion."

I point to the bed that pulls down and becomes one of the two sleepers.

"You can take a nap up there if you want," I say.

"Planning on playing any of your songs to me?" she says.

"Ouch. Want something to drink?"

"Have I wanted something since you've met me?"

"There's always a first."

"No."

I mix Sprite with a tiny bottle of rum I received on my last flight. The attendant had said she felt sorry I was so worried about the turbulence. So half a dozen of these suckers were my parting gift.

"Is there anywhere you don't drink?" Cara asks me as I sit down across from her.

"The shower. Most of the time."

We banter back and forth like this until about ten minutes later when there's another knock on the door. I raise my fist in the air and pump it as I stand and open the curtain.

A look of horror and abandonment faces us.

"Can I help you?" I ask Molly.

She moves her head and sees Cara sitting there. Cara waves at her.

"Oh, I'm sorry."

"We just want a little privacy, if you don't mind."

"No, not at all." She waits for a moment, then says, "How long will you want that?"

"Until we reach California," I say.

"Aren't you just going to Oklahoma?"

"Have a great day."

"It's almost evening," she says as I slide the curtain back in place.

I stand there but don't hear footsteps walking away.

"Is she for real?" Cara whispers.

I nod. "Oh, yeah. The stories I could tell you about stalkers."

She shakes her head. "And here I thought you really just wanted my company."

"Nah," I joke. "Couldn't be that."

I'm listening to my iPod and watching Cara sleep across from me with her head leaning toward the window. It's fun to just study her. When she's not babbling on about something and moving with her nervous energy, she's actually quite attractive. She has this peaceful look about her, this innocent look that seems real. I wonder what it'd be like waking up with that look facing me on a pillow next to mine.

I wonder what it'd be like to have someone like Cara in my life.

Enough. Stop that.

I just swatted myself with a flyswatter, kinda like my grandma used to do whenever we kids were misbehaving. Cara is really cute and it's really sweet to think about all that, but cute and sweet went out of my life when my ex Reilly took them with her.

I quickly turn up the music. I'm listening to Electric Light Orchestra's greatest hits. It's a fun and upbeat set of tunes, and it seems to fit this experience. It seems to fit Cara. I couldn't find any Michael Jackson or Prince on my iPod, so this will have to do.

I secretly want Jeff Lynne to produce my next album. My love of the frontman of Electric Light Orchestra and the famous producer who has worked with everybody from the Beatles to Tom Petty is widely documented, but I want to do an album with him. Of course, I might end up coming off sounding more like George Harrison (who he produced) than George Jones. Country music is ready for a lot of things, but this . . . well, yeah.

I think of things like this. To shake things up and get people going, "Huh?"

Sometimes in the middle of the night or the early morning (whatever normal people call it—it's been a long time since I've been normal), I break out a little gem of an album like *Out of the Blue*. It's brilliant and bold and, yeah, it's blue. It's blue in all the ways blue can be. Bright sky blue and melancholy deep blue and blue as—

Whoa.

I almost just said, "Cara's eyes." What's wrong with me?

I don't know. I really don't know.

I haven't told my manager about the Jeff Lynne idea, the same way I haven't told him about the Rick Rubin idea. That's a little more digestible, since Rubin is one of a handful of the greatest producers ever (Johnny Cash, anybody?). But still.

Lynne and Rubin aren't Heath Sawyer producers. That's not my sound or my brand or my business.

Which is exactly why I say bring them on and shake up expectations.

It's a nice thought. Sorta like Cara's eyes.

A nice, sweet thought that doesn't fit and never will. The guitars are different and the beats are different and the whole vibe is completely different.

Are you talking about Rick Rubin or Cara?

I don't know. Both. And thinking of both of them is funny. To me.

She's still asleep in the seat across from me, and I wonder what she's dreaming about. I know she's not thinking of music producers. Maybe she's dreaming about mathematics. Not sure how that would go, but perhaps numbers are swimming and riding and running all alongside her. Equations she can't get rid of, the same way it is with melodies for me. Perhaps she's still doing accounting in her sleep, which is terribly ironic because I failed that class in college.

I should stop this producer-thinking business because I still need to get some songs picked out to record for next year's Christmas album. So sorry, Brian Eno and Dr. Dre. You'll have to wait.

For a lifetime. Whatever that looks like.

I stare at the figure with the face looking so serene and so sweet.

Yeah. Some things just don't belong together. Like sweet accountants and stranded country musicians.

The Christmas your grandmother passed away—my mother—was tough on all of us. Especially me. She had always been such an unwavering presence in our family. And she so dearly loved you. Like everybody else, she loved to laugh with you and at you. She would never get to see what happened and how the rest of the world discovered your talents. Sometimes I wonder if she's watching over you, helping those tight doors open and helping nudge you through them.

CHAPTER FOURTEEN

The Christmas Waltz

$\mathcal{O}$ne of the lights above the doorway has turned on since the world outside has turned dark. I think we have another hour or so to go before we reach Kansas City. Cara has just bought a Diet Pepsi to wake herself up before we change trains.

"We're almost there," she says, as she yawns and stretches.

"I love how I put you to sleep," I say.

"I'm sorry—I didn't mean to nod off."

"I'm kidding. Hey—at least I wasn't playing you one of my songs."

She glances at the magazine I was browsing through when she woke up. "*Country Weekly?* Can I take a look at that?"

"Sure thing."

"Are you in here?"

"Yeah, I think so."

She finds a piece that has musicians talking about their

fondest Christmas memories. I'm quoted as recalling shooting a deer and then eating him later that day.

"Did that really happen?"

"Sure it did," I say. "What, you think I'm just making that up?"

"Yeah."

"What you see is what you get."

I watch her thumbing through the magazine, talking about people she's never heard of and then others that she knows.

"Isn't he married to the woman that used to be married to some big-name actor?"

I shake my head. "Pop culture just isn't your thing, is it?"

"I like watching the red carpet things before award shows."

"They do those at the CMAs, you know."

"The what?" Cara asks.

"The Country Music Awards."

"Ah." She gets to the page on me. "'Heath Sawyer Isn't Looking for Love.' Ooh, I think I want to read this article."

There's really nothing much to read. It shows me at various events with a few ladies I've brought, including of course my "on-again-off-again girlfriend Naomi Parks," according to the magazine.

"Wow—she's like a goddess," Cara says. "Is she a super-model?"

"In her head," I say.

"So—let me guess—you guys are currently off again."

"I just enrolled in the never-again plan. It's working out quite well."

"She's gorgeous."

"Douse her with a bucket of water and then say that."

I'm being a bit cynical 'cause Naomi is absolutely hot. But those genes will only get her so far. She won't be young and gorgeous all her life. But something tells me she'll be crazy for the rest of it.

"Here's a nice quote," Cara says, reading out loud. "'Now is about the last time for me to settle down. I'm too busy to know where I'm going to be tomorrow. Imagine taking care of a kid in that world.'"

I just smile and nod.

"I bet Naomi loved that quote."

"She actually probably does. She wants kids less than I do."

"So did you always know you wanted to do this?" she says, handing me back the magazine.

"It's all I've ever been really good at. I started playing and performing when I was a teenager. My parents encouraged me. It all came pretty easy for me."

"So no long and hard road you had to travel?"

The steady motion of the train is almost soothing. Cara looks different in the dim light of this sleeper compartment.

"Nah, it all happened fast. I mean—don't get me wrong, I've worked my tail off. But it's just been in the last year when it all exploded. It's all relative, though. Lots of people haven't heard of me." I clear my throat in an obnoxious way.

"I'm probably in the minority."

"For living in Oklahoma, yeah," I admit.

"Is it all—you know—what you might think it would be? I mean—I know that's such a stupid and clichéd question, but I've always wondered. I've always wanted to ask some big-name celebrity. Is it better than you thought it would be or is it worse?"

"Oh, it's pretty awesome," I say. "Parts, that is. The perks. The privileges, you know. But it's sorta like this. We're on this train riding in this car. I feel like my career is that way. It's like this beast in the same small room as I am and it never goes away. It's a beast that has to be fed."

"Are you calling me a beast?"

"Absolutely." I laugh. "Want a candy bar?"

Cara tries to roar and it comes out sounding like a frog.

"That's the saddest roar I've ever heard."

"Yeah, I know, right? Pathetic."

"You know something?" I say. "You're real. I like that. I mean—girls like Naomi—I could spend a hundred more years with her and still not really know her. Still not really *get* her. But it just seems like—it feels like I've known you for a long time."

"Are you saying I look old?"

"Nah. I'm just saying—I don't have many longtime friends. At least none I hang out with anymore on a regular basis."

"Well, I can always be your train buddy. And anytime you need someone to hold your hand on the plane."

"You did that before you knew exactly who I was."

A playful grin fills her face. "Do you need me to hold your hand again?"

"Maybe," I say, trying to be all sly and cool.

The word seems to hover over us, and then both of our isn't-this-cute-talk looks go away. I see the real look on the woman across from me. It's not playful, nor is it sweet.

It's the look of someone who might be skydiving for the first time.

"You know, Cara, I just want you to—"

The train's horn bellows, several times, over and over again, and then we feel a giant jerk. The train lurches front and back and seems to shake and possibly go off the rails. I see Cara's hand grab the arm of her chair. The horns keep blaring and the train starts to slow down.

"Wow, they must've heard you talking," I say as I look outside. I don't see anything.

"Are we there?"

"No. Something happened. It's like—it felt like we hit something."

Then I look out and see the shadow of what looks like a mangled truck on its side at the edge of the road. A red sign on top of its roof says JOEY'S PIZZA. It looks like a pizza delivery truck.

I can only imagine who was behind the wheel. And what the poor guy's obituary is going to say.

Died while delivering a pepperoni pizza on Christmas Eve.

You were fifteen when you decided you really wanted to pursue this music thing. And that was when I finally agreed and began to help. I remember Christmas that year, buying you music lessons and seeing your disappointment. You thought you didn't need lessons—you could already play well enough. You wanted to perform; you didn't want to learn. Those lessons never even got finished. You were right—you didn't need them. Sometimes you just learn things on your own by doing them. That's the story of your life.

CHAPTER FIFTEEN

Santa Baby

I stand and survey the scene. Somebody above is playing a joke on me. Or maybe it's the other way around. Maybe I'm getting a little of what I deserve.

Snow is flying every which way I can see. The wind seems to pierce you deep down inside. People are roaming around trying to figure out what to do and where to go and how they're going to get to their destination now that we've been told the train is not starting up again. After an attendant on the train came out and told us what had happened, half of the passengers seemed deaf and dumb and blind because they're still acting like the train is about to start up again.

"So the train idea really was a good one, huh?" Cara says in utter astonishment as her hair whips around like a tornado.

We've walked in the snow until reaching a barely plowed road where the accident occurred. Can I call it an accident? I'm not sure, since the train basically mangled a truck delivering pizzas. And the driver?

Well, it looks like the police are talking to him right now.

"There's no way . . ." I can't say anything more.

Standing there between a couple of cops is Santa Claus. Well, Santa if Santa had half his beard hanging off his very bald head. Headlights from the cop cars illuminate the scene. Santa looks like he just escaped from either prison or the nuthouse.

"Is that the driver?" Cara asks above the noise of the wind.

It doesn't look like Santa can stand up very well.

Are times so hard that every Santa around is in really, really bad shape?

"Hey, Maw," I say in the best backwoods redneck hillbilly accent I can muster, "the good news is that Daddy is alive. The bad news is he got fired from delivering pizzas as Santa."

"Who eats pizza on Christmas Eve?" Cara asks.

I laugh in disbelief. "A drunken Santa gets his truck creamed by an Amtrak train and you wonder who's eating pizza on Christmas Eve."

"Well, it is a bit strange, isn't it?"

"I think I'm being haunted."

"By who?"

"By the ghost of Santas past or something like that. Maybe they're all trying to prevent me from getting home."

Cara is holding her suitcase, which she'd kept with her.

"They said buses are going to come in a minute," she says.

"And bring us where?" The sky is dark and black trees surround us. "Where'd he say we were?"

"We're about ten minutes from Carrollton, Missouri. That's about an hour and a half from Kansas City."

"I'm never getting home."

"Sure you will," Cara says over the howling wind. "It might be January third when you do, but you'll get home."

My emotions are competing. There's the humorous don't-give-a-rip emotion circling up high. Then there's the odd lost-in-a-*Twilight-Zone*-Christmas-episode feeling in my gut. Then in a darker place, there's this is-somebody-out-to-get-me sense of dread deep down inside.

"You okay?" Cara asks.

"I don't know. I should've stayed in New York."

"Oh, come on. Look at the Missouri countryside."

There's nothing around us but trees and rolling hills and darkness.

"If I drove a pizza truck around here, I'd stop it on the tracks too," I say.

"Cut it out," Cara says. "Drunken Santa might be going through hard times. Hey—you should go up to him and say hi."

"Yeah, that worked out so well last time I did it. And I'm telling you—if it's the same Santa following us, I'm going to get far, far away from you."

"From me? What do I have to do with this?"

"Maybe you're like an omen, or you have some kinda voo-doo hex on you."

"You're more likely to have that than I am."

I decide to forgo saying hi to Santa. Soon several buses come to pick up the stranded passengers to take us to Carroll-ton, where . . . where we'll hang out in Carrollton. No offense to Carrollton, which I'm sure is a sweet little town. It's just that I need to be in another sweet little town in a different state right about now.

Cara makes a funny face at me as I sit next to her on the bus.

"What's that?"

"*That* is what you're doing right now. Smile. At least our train didn't derail. At least we're still alive."

I look over and see a very large woman in sweatpants trying her hardest to adjust them. But it looks like they're five sizes too small, and unfortunately, she's showing quite a bit more than anybody would like to see. She tries for, like, a minute, and then the struggle just seems too hard, so she gives up.

Someone passes us smelling like—smelling really, really bad. Like they were running alongside the train until it stopped.

I force a smile and say to Cara, "Yeah, this is wonderful. How far is that town?"

"Carrollton is ten minutes away."

"Yeah, but we're already at Crazytown."

I'm waiting in a bus station for our bags to be delivered. I'm in the corner in a seat and have been keeping a low profile. I'm wearing a cap, but it doesn't really do much good. Every few minutes someone says hi or takes my picture or strikes up a conversation. Right now at this point in my wonderful trip home, I don't want to talk to anybody. The joke is over and I just want to get home. I know Momma's gonna be worried and I'm going to be stuck and the worst thing is that there's not even a bar around to be stuck in.

I'd love to blame this on someone, but there's nobody I can blame it on. Except maybe Cara, but that's ridiculous because she's gotten me this far.

Maybe she really is a bad-luck charm. No joke.

But there's no reason we need to separate now.

It's not like you're traveling home with her, you idiot.

That's true. But a part of me fears having to figure stuff out on my own if she disappears. And it's not just that. I genuinely enjoy her company.

"They're not telling us anything."

I've been scrolling through Facebook on my phone, and the voice shocks me. I'd recognize that deadpan sound anywhere.

"Hello," I tell Molly.

"Did you lose her?"

"Excuse me?"

"Your lady friend."

"She's around."

And hopefully coming back.

"I just wanted to tell you something," she says in the most robotic voice I've ever heard. "You have really nice skin."

I nod and force a smile and feel the goose bumps come out on that really nice skin. I might have a lot of nice things, but my *skin* isn't one of them.

"So where are you heading later tonight?" Molly asks.

I look down and notice that Molly has different-colored socks on. I'm not about to ask if she did this on purpose or not.

"I, uh, need to make a call. Can you excuse me?"

She nods and then stands there. For a second I wait and then I start dialing a number. A made-up number. She eventually leaves me be.

Cara comes walking back to the seat. "Well, we're in luck."

"We?"

"Oh, excuse me. Well, *I'm* in luck. And I'll hear about your missing body on the news tomorrow during my Christmas lunch in Tulsa."

"Please make a toast to me then."

"Seriously—I have a ride for us to Kansas City, if you want."

"Let me guess—by bus? But it's full of preschool children and the driver is Santa Claus?"

"No. It might be worse. It's my cousin Pervis. I haven't seen him in a long time. He's a bit—squirrelly."

"Oh, come on," I say, leaning back in this uncomfortable seat. "That's really his name? Pervis?"

"Yes."

"Sounds like *pervert*. Or something worse."

"You really are in sixth grade, aren't you? Guys all have a one-track mind, don't they?"

"Yep. Even if Santa tries to derail them. They're just always the same. Boobs and beer and fart jokes."

"Well, *Pervis* can take us to Kansas City. If you'd like."

"How long do we have?"

"Why?"

"There's a bar right next door," I tell her.

I smile. She sighs.

The story of our relationship so far.

I think we all knew that Christmas, the last one of your high school years. We just all seemed to feel that this was the last time we'd all be together like this. The girls were in college, and you were planning on heading to Nashville, and the future looked bright. We believed because you believed. We still didn't know the road ahead—who could have known? Nobody knows until they venture out. A part of me was afraid 'cause I didn't want to let you go.

CHAPTER SIXTEEN

Blue Christmas

"So why did things suddenly take off for you this year?" Cara asks from across the small table where we're sitting.

"It's my irresistible charm," I joke.

We're at the bar in a little joint that has suddenly been invaded by people from the train. Thirsty people. Nobody's bothering us, which I'm thankful for. I've actually convinced Cara to get a beer herself.

"Okay, seriously," she says, not liking my answer.

"I'm bein' serious. Hey—the fans love me. Those who know me."

"I'd heard about you. I just didn't recognize you. There's a difference."

"Oh, so if I'd said, 'Hi, I'm Heath Sawyer,' you would have then given me a little respect?"

"I was in a men's restroom at the airport with a carafe of

coffee spilled all over me," she says. "So, yeah, probably not. And am I giving you respect now? Because if you think I am, I must be giving you the wrong impression or something."

She's starting to give as good as she gets.

"You asked earlier whether it had been a long hard road. I got acceptance in this industry early on. But my career has been a lesson in how not to do it. A picture of total and complete persistence. I'm just too dang stubborn to let it go."

"To let what go?"

I shrug and finish my beer. "Everything. Country music and fame and songwriting and movies and all that."

"But did everything suddenly explode in just the last year?"

"I remember this one moment—a third single off my fourth album suddenly went nowhere—and I was thinking, 'This might really be it. I might really be done.' But I remember the moment I just said, 'No. It ain't happenin'.' Nobody else— nobody, and I mean *nobody*—was there saying, 'Go, Heath, go.' Nope. It was just me. And a lot of people don't like being that one lone figure. A lot of people hate that. Most people go with the flow. They're spoon-fed. But not me. I tossed the spoon out the window years ago."

"Tossed the spoon, huh?"

"That's a figure of speech," I say with a grin.

"I gathered that," she replies with a beautiful grin herself.

I think for a second, then quickly add, "You know, I take that back. What I said. My parents were there saying, 'Go, Heath, go.' I take them for granted. Well, I should say I take my mother for granted, since my father is no longer around."

I order another round even though she still has most of her first beer left.

"You hear enough success stories, and they all turn out to be the same. You have some talent and some total cluelessness added into some dumb luck and some right-place-right-time. Then you sprinkle in unique personalities and watch out. Every now and then you just become fortunate, and that's where I'm at right now. A lot of wrong roads and dead-end streets until you find a shortcut to an expressway."

"So why don't you use that ability and find us an expressway?"

"I was following you."

"And look where that led us."

"I don't mind this," I tell her.

"Yeah, 'cause you're in a bar and you're already finished with your second round."

"Exactly."

But she knows there's more to this moment, and it includes her sitting there next to me.

It might be easy to examine what's happening here, but I'm not going to. I'm just going to try to enjoy the moment and not think too hard about tomorrow or next week or next year.

Tomorrow is Christmas Day. Maybe you should be thinking about that a little harder.

"Want to do a shot?" I ask her.

"Absolutely not."

I order two shots in case she changes her mind.

"What is that?"

"Whiskey."

She groans.

"It goes well with beer. Ever hear of a boilermaker?"

"Ever hear of AA?"

I laugh, but she doesn't laugh with me. I take the shot, then follow it with the beer.

"'Tis the season," I tell her.

"That's what you probably say every day, huh?"

"Look—*Pervis* is gonna come soon, and I have a feeling I need a few of those before seeing him."

She flips back her ponytail in an anxious manner, as if her mind is running a million miles a second. "He's a good guy. Just—eccentric."

I hear a Christmas song by a country music singer. It reminds me of the album I'm supposed to be thinking about and planning for.

"So tell me about you," I say. "I've spent all this time talking about me. What's your story?"

She shifts in her chair. "I don't have a story."

"Everybody has a story. Some just don't write songs about it."

Suddenly, everything changes. A switch turns off. A power source shuts down.

"Hey—what? What'd I say?"

"Nothing." Her voice is turned way, way down. She stares straight ahead, even though there's nothing much to look at there.

"Wait—I know I say dumb things, but what'd I say now? What? Did you have someone just die in your family?"

Her head shakes and she finishes her drink. For a second I see her take her finger and circle the top of her glass.

"You're a foreign spy," I say.

"What?"

"Okay, just a joke to relieve the tension. I'm not claiming it was a good one."

"'A foreign spy.' Yeah, not the best joke."

"A C at best."

"A D-plus," Cara says.

"I'm just— The whole let's-talk-about-being-a-famous-singer thing gets old, I'm sure. I just wanted to talk about you."

"So talk."

"I mean I wanted *you* to talk about you. Your family."

She takes a long sip from her second beer, and I watch in strange admiration. She finishes half of it there in a way that says she's partied before. Her eyes become glassy and I wonder if she's feeling anything from the drink and a half she's had. But I don't know. I have no idea, since I've been drinking all my life.

"You want to know what it's like? Trying being the Super Glue that's never supposed to run out. That's never supposed to get sticky. That's always supposed to keep things held together. That's supposed to be invisible and foolproof and wonderful and amazing and—"

She puts two hands in front of her face, and then I think she starts to cry.

"Whoa—hold up here. Okay. Happy time. Breathe in. Just—slow down."

I can see her body shaking. This is just—unexpected.

You don't need another head case to deal with.

But I shush that voice up, because this is a different kind of head case. If Cara can actually be called one.

"Forget I asked," I tell her.

"I can't forget because they're there morning, noon, and night. And I just—sometimes, I swear. It's like, I just pray that I can make it through a whole day before something or someone breaks."

I glance around the bar to see if anybody is eavesdropping, but we're being left alone.

"That bad, huh?" I ask.

Cara puts two fingers on a shot glass. "You know—I made a deal with God. I told Him I'd be responsible if He just looked after my brother. And I've upheld my part of the bargain."

She drains the shot and I see her eyes water up again. She shakes her head and squints.

"Not so smooth, huh?"

Cara looks at me with eyes different from the ones I've been seeing. These look weighed down and afraid, but mostly they look real.

"Nothing's ever smooth in my life. My brother is a mess, and now I'm wondering how I can try to take care of him while being there for my family."

Her phone lights up. Gotta love timing like this.

It's her cousin Pervis. She takes the call and listens and then thanks him.

"He's almost here. A couple of minutes. Just wait."

She stands and wipes her face and doesn't look at me. I move and stand directly in front of her so I can look down at her.

"Are you okay?" I ask.

"Are you? Is anybody? I mean, really? I think the only people who say they're okay are the ones who are insane. Or have Alzheimer's."

"Wow. You're a sad drunk."

"I'm not drunk," Cara states in a loud voice.

"Yeah, I know. But liquor does different things to different people. You—it seems to make you sad."

"All it does is take off the mask," she says.

"That's funny, 'cause all it does to me is put the mask back on."

"Look at us. We're playing Halloween and it's Christmas Eve."

"And we're putting our lives in the hands of . . . Pervis."

I say his name with as much dramatic effect as I can. It inspires a laugh. That's all I wanted.

"Cara—listen. I don't know you. Not that well. But as for being the Super Glue—you do a pretty good job with it."

She sighs and her body seems half the size that it was just a moment ago. "I'm just tired of being the Super Glue."

I chuckle. "I'm just tired of being super."

"How about if neither of us tries to be anything super the rest of tonight?" she says.

"Sounds good to me. I mean—I know I can't do anything about my super good looks."

"Or your super tall tales," she says.

"You're very right."

Even though you'd only been gone for half a year, I still had to persuade you to come back to Oklahoma for Christmas that year. You were so busy and so determined to "make it." I had to remind you that coming back home would be good for your heart and for your soul. I still have to remind you. There really, truly is no place like home.

CHAPTER SEVENTEEN

Sleigh Ride

'm picturing a totally skinny redneck with oversized eyes and teeth who can barely hold a conversation. Instead, Pervis shows up looking nothing like I thought he would.

"I'm Heath," I tell him as I shake his hand.

"Yes, I'm aware of who you are," the short, curly-haired, glasses-wearing redhead tells me.

He looks like a computer geek, not a hillbilly.

"Hello, Cara," he says in a formal and weird way.

"Would you like a drink?" I ask him.

"No, I do not partake of alcoholic beverages."

"Want a soft drink? Anything? A bite to eat?"

I'm just trying to be nice.

"We should get going. I have an online game session at ten fifteen tonight."

"Thank you so much for coming to get us," Cara says. "I didn't know what to do. I know it's Christmas Eve."

"I'm surprised you're actually rushing back home to see your family," he says as we follow him out of the bar.

Cara looks at me but doesn't say anything.

"How are the roads?" I ask before we get outside.

"How do you think they are?"

Maybe everybody in their family just has something against me. Perhaps my great-great-grandfather shot their great-great-grandfather. I don't know. I don't get it.

"Well, good thing you managed to get here."

"I have four-wheel drive," Pervis says.

I initially pictured a big ol' truck, but not for this Pervis. His SUV is neat and tidy, like his haircut and glasses. Cara tells me to get in the front, but I'd rather not. I'd rather go in the back, in the trunk. Somehow I still end up in the seat next to good ol' Pervis.

"I hear the conditions are a lot worse where you guys are headed," he says to us as he pulls out of the parking lot.

"That's encouraging," I say with a laugh.

"Just wanted to let you know. Not sure if you heard the weather reports while you were boozing it up in the bar."

"I blame your cousin," I tell him.

Pervis nods and gets onto a freeway that's not too bad. Snow is still falling hard, thick flakes drifting sideways. But plows have done a good job on this road.

"So are you having sexual relations with Cara?"

The question is so unreal that I stop and really have to wonder if I imagined it. Not just the question itself, but how he said it. How he phrased it.

"Pervis!" Cara shoves his shoulder.

"You know, she *is* in the backseat," I say.

"I just want to know."

"Yes, we are," I say. "And it's crazy intense. Like so, so hot."

"Stop it! No, Pervis, we're not, and get your mind out of the gutter."

"How many times have you heard that line?" I ask him, assuming he's heard it a million times. 'Cause of his name.

"What do you mean?"

Jeez.

I'm surprised Pervis isn't wearing a Santa hat, because it's just my luck. Just my wonderful luck. Pervis the driver.

Ten minutes into the trip, after Pervis and Cara catch up and I'm left thankfully alone, the driver tries to find a weather report on the radio. He turns to a station playing a great new song by one of my favorite singers out there. Reba still sounds great and always will.

Pervis grimaces and changes the station.

"That woman can sing," I say.

"Tell me one good thing about country," Pervis says in a snotty little voice.

I'm feeling the shot inside of me. I'm also feeling like this short red rascal oughta see the side of my boot.

"It just feels good."

"Every single song is utter cliché," he says, facing straight ahead, not even bothering to look me in the eye when he says that.

"A lot of clichés are that way because they're the truth."

"The truth? Country music is 'the truth'? Are you joking?"

"Pervis . . ."

Cara is in the backseat not knowing what to do. Then again, she always seems to be a little uneasy saying his name.

"I'm not trying to be rude," the driver says. "I'm just being real."

I've gotten into this conversation many times before. Granted, I haven't talked about this with a complete stranger in a very long time.

"You know the good thing about my songs? They don't make you feel bad."

"You ever watch the news?"

"Yeah. And that's why I don't want to feel bad." I pause for a minute and once again try to be friendly. "So what profession are you in?"

"I write video games."

"You write the software on the games or the actual story-lines?"

"Please," he says, still not looking at me, still fascinated by the highway straight ahead of him. "I'd be bored out of my mind implementing code all day."

"So what if I said, 'Tell me one good thing about video games'?"

"Do you have an hour? I could give you a hundred. They can expand your mind."

"A video game?" I ask. "Really?"

"I know that's a little eye-opening to an old-timer like you."

I gotta laugh. I turn around and see Cara just shake her head.

"Did you tell him to be this way?"

"Cara didn't have to say anything," Pervis says. "She knows me. She knows I speak my mind."

"So what kind of music do you like?" I ask him.

"Take a guess."

Well, we're not in New York. He might not be following his family roots and sticking with country, but there's no way this kid is into the hipster stuff I just left back in the Big Apple. He's got anger and he's got a fight to pick and he's got short-guy syndrome. Let's see.

"Metallica," I tell him.

"Oh, please," he says. "Talk about cliché."

"No?"

"Sure, yeah, back when they were something."

Yep. I'm right. Heavy metal, hard rock, however you want to call it.

"I like 'Nothing Else Matters,' " I say.

"Of course you do. A bunch of head cases they are. There are lots of other, better bands."

"There always are," I say.

I've always said this when someone has questioned my rise to fame. *How'd you get so big, Heath Sawyer? How'd you do it?* Because, sometimes, even when they don't seem to be saying it, they seem to imply, *How in the heck did YOU get here? 'Cause Jim Bob is so much more talented. And Joe Mama is such a better singer. And June Bug is so much better-looking.*

"Listen to this," Pervis says. "Now this is music. The first time I heard these guys . . ."

He goes on a rant for about five minutes and puts in some heavy metal that sounds really bad. I just nod and pretend to listen, but I know there's no way he's going to listen to a word I say. About anything. I'm surprised he picked me up. Then again, maybe he picked us up specifically to make this declaration in his car. It's happened before.

People take their music seriously. And that's okay. I get that.

You used to take it seriously before the business sucked it up.

"Nothing Else Matters" seems very appropriate right about now. I wish I could hear it, because I love not only the music but the lyrics. There's nothing clichéd about them. This was a band hitting it at the right time with the right music and the right lyrics and the right *everything*. And when that happens, nothing else truly matters. The world embraces them and they suddenly become something else. They no longer belong to themselves. They are forever others'. Forever a part of the rest of the world.

"Maybe I'm not like the rest of them," I tell Pervis.

"Oh, you're like them."

"Why are you being so mean?" Cara asks.

"This isn't being mean. This is being honest. This is a good-looking guy who can sing nice songs and smile pretty for the camera. Of course someone like me who burns in the sun after being outside for, like, five minutes is predetermined to hate a Heath Sawyer, but I'm not. It's not that silly stuff. It's because he chooses—*chooses*—to make obvious career decisions."

This guy has got some guts. I gotta give him that.

"They're not all that obvious, brother," I tell him.

"Of course they are. Listen, the next thing you're going to do is come out with a Christmas album."

I look at him and can't help but bust out laughing. This is good. No, not good. This is great. This is beautiful. Honesty.

This is so far from the masses singing the songs and looking at you like you're part of the set decoration.

After I've spent nine months on the road, forgetting what it's like to make myself some toast, the edge on Pervis is strangely welcome.

"Cara, I think I like your cousin."

"I think *my cousin* is being a royal jerk. Even if he's just 'speaking his mind.'"

"And is that anything new?" Pervis asks her.

He really is a mousy sort of inquisitive nerd type. He's the guy who would press the buttons on the end-of-the-world nukes if he could. He'd have a justification why. It's all about being logical and sensible. Forget people and how they feel. If you're driving a country music star to a city in the middle of a blizzard on Christmas Eve and you feel like country music is garbage, then you gotta tell that country musician.

"You know what I like about you?" I tell him.

"My cheekbones?"

I laugh. "Well, your sense of humor, for one. But also this honesty. I like it."

"I'm sorry," Cara says.

"Don't be. Pervis, did you have plans tonight?"

"Yes. Some online gaming."

"See?" I turn around and say to Cara. "This guy is taking time out of his schedule for us."

"It's really just for her," Pervis says.

"Okay, then, just for you. And I don't blame him. I'd drive you across the state on Christmas Eve if you asked me."

"I might be asking you in about an hour, you know?" she says.

A moment later, Pervis puts a disk in. The most annoying sound ever comes out of the speakers.

"Nice Christmas songs," I say.

"This is Misery Train."

"You got that right," I mumble.

"What?"

The music is blaring now.

"I said this is wild."

Somewhere, not far away, is a two-story Victorian home lit up with wreaths and lights where my mother and sisters and their families are celebrating. Maybe listening to Christmas songs. Opening a single present as is the tradition. Perhaps laughing and eating and playing games. Maybe watching *It's a Wonderful Life*.

I'm stuck on a Misery Train and don't see any signs of life. The snow is getting worse. The roads are getting worse. And the sound track is definitely getting way, way, *way* worse.

If a guardian angel were to come down and rescue me, his name would be George. George Jones.

The year you came back home and gave up your dreams was a difficult one. Nothing your father or I could say or do would change you. Three long and hard years had changed you. That silly boy who thought he could conquer the world had come back different. Those nine months you were back home—I still think those were nine of the best months of my life. I still believed. I still somehow knew. Success was right around the corner.

CHAPTER EIGHTEEN

Little Donkey

"*Y*our train *hit* a car?"

"A pizza delivery truck," I tell my sister Karen. She's already spent the last ten minutes laughing.

"But the guy was okay?"

"He was dressed as a Santa. You tell me if he's okay. We gotta look up online and see if he went to jail. People were furious at him."

"That had to make the evening news."

"I got out of there fast 'cause I didn't want to show up on it. Can you imagine? 'Heath Sawyer rides train that hits pizza delivery guy.'"

"Yes," Karen says. "It would be very fitting. People would think they're making it up."

"Yeah—this whole trip has been one big PR stunt."

I glance at Pervis, who ignores my comment. He's driving

to an address I gave him for a rental car company. The snow hasn't relented a bit.

"There's no way you're going to be able to make it tonight, Heath."

"I'll make it."

"The roads are awful. It's the only thing they're talking about. They were shutting some of them down around Tulsa."

"I'll rent a big ol' truck and plow my way home."

"Aw, man, this sucks."

"Yeah, I know." I knew this call would produce some guilt.

"No, it's that . . ." Karen's voice fades away.

"What is it?"

"Mom wanted all of us here tomorrow morning."

"Okay. She always does."

"No—it's for something else. Something she has planned."

Karen is the worst about keeping secrets. She's never been able to, at least not from me.

"What? What's she have planned?"

"You have to swear—Heath, I mean it, you can't tell her you know."

"Know what?"

"She got us all special gifts. That's all I'll say. Not just regular gifts. Stuff she's been working on. For a while. And Mom asked for help on yours."

"Oh, man."

"What?" Karen asks.

"I don't want Christmas morning to become some big sob-fest. And I know it's going to. Just like the funeral."

"Well, you won't be here."

"I'll be there. I have to be there. I don't want the guilt treatment I'll get from all of you if I'm not."

"We don't give you guilt."

"Are you kidding? Please. It's gonna be brutal."

"We can open presents later in the day," Karen says.

"You know how Momma is about traditions."

There is a pause. I hear Pervis mumble something about missing a turn.

"This isn't going to be the traditional Christmas," Karen says.

"I know. That's why I gotta get home."

"Well, just don't you get hurt tryin' to make it home, you hear me?"

"Yes, second mom."

I tell Karen good-bye. In a lot of ways, all my sisters were motherly types to me. I was raised not by one woman but by four of them. All different and stubborn and strong-willed and loving me in their own unique ways.

Pervis stops the car in front of a darkened building. It's nine thirty. Nothing about this looks promising.

"Uh, yeah, I told you. Nobody's there."

"Let's get closer to the airport."

"That's on the other side of town," he says.

"Look, I'll pay you for your time."

"You can't put a price tag on my time," Pervis says.

"How about two hundred bucks plus I'll fill your tank of gas before we leave?"

"Deal."

* * *

The SUV slides and spins for a moment seconds after I get back inside.

"That's the third rental car place we've checked out," Pervis says as he swipes the curb of the parking lot heading back out onto the street.

"There might not be any open." Cara's still in the backseat, holding on to the armrest on the door.

"We'll find one," I say, thumbing through the list on my phone. "Just let me keep trying to make some calls."

"We might be stuck here," Cara says.

I first look at her, then at Pervis.

No. No way I'm stuck with this guy on Christmas Eve. Uh-uh.

"We'll get something."

"I just think they're closed because of the storm," Cara says. "And since it's Christmas Eve."

I curse and keep looking on my phone. I find an address and number that says "Mike Rentals." I call, not expecting anything but instead I actually get a living, breathing human. Well, not sure if he's living or breathing, but he is talking.

"Yeah."

"Is this Mike?"

"No."

"Is Mike there?"

The man laughs. "It's Mike Rentals. Not Mike's Rentals."

"Are you guys open?"

"You wanna rent a vehicle now?"

"Yes."

"You plannin' on sledding down a mountain or something?"

I seriously think every single person I've spoken to in the last couple of days has been a smart-ass out to get me.

"I just need a car."

"Well, we got 'em. Not sure how far you'll get in this blizzard, however."

"Do you know of any other rental places open?"

"Oh, yeah, I know about a dozen. Can I text their numbers to your phone?"

Wise guy. I swear. Every single person.

"Doubt any of them are open anyway," Wise Guy says.

"Okay, but you're open, right?"

"It's just me. I'm open whenever someone needs a car."

I pause for a minute as the lights of the Kansas City Airport shimmer in the distance. "Do you rent from your garage?"

"Nah, man. I got a lot of Mikes."

He's got a lot of Mikes. What does that even mean?

"Okay, I'll be there in about ten minutes or so. Just—stay there, okay?"

I give Pervis the address and tell him what the directions on my phone say, then tell Cara we're in business.

"I can't believe someone's still open," she says.

"People will always need cars to rent," I say. "So someone's going to be willing to take their money."

A small fenced-in lot stands next to a small one-story house. In front of it is the tiniest car I've ever seen.

No, that's not a car. That would make a go-kart look big.

"What is this place?" Cara asks.

"Oh, yeah, I've heard of stuff like this."

"What do you mean, 'stuff like this'?" I ask Pervis.

"Haven't you heard of a Mike car? Micro. It's one of those

green cars. It's new. Big in Canada. The mileage is supposed to be incredible."

"A kid hiccupping would knock that thing over," I say.

The lot is full of snow-covered cars the same exact size. The size of my thumb. Mileage is the absolute last thing I'm thinking of.

Mike Rentals. I'm renting a micro car.

"That's like a clown car," I tell them.

"Some things are just meant to be," Pervis says.

I let out a deliberately fake laugh. I really don't like this guy. That's the only reason I get out of his SUV. I just want to be away from Pervis. Even if I have to drive a circus car.

I knock on the door of the house and a guy wearing a long robe comes out. The wind seems to swirl around us as we stand there talking. It's obvious after a couple of minutes that he's not going to let me in his house.

"Tell me you have something bigger," I say.

"Naw, man."

"Do you really rent those?"

"Sure I do. I used to have an ostrich business, but that didn't work out too well."

And this is your next business venture? Wonderful.

I shake my head. It's freezing out here.

"Can we go inside for a moment?" I ask.

He just shakes his head. "The lady doesn't want to be bothered, if you know what I mean."

I don't know what he means and I'm afraid to ask. He tells me he'll need a credit card and my license. I'm almost afraid to hand them over. I see the half of his hair that was covering his bald spot suddenly blowing to the side.

"Are you on TV?" he asks.

"Uh, no. I mean—not really."

"You look familiar."

"I have that kind of face," I say, another line I'm used to using.

It's dark outside and I'm still wearing my Bud cap, so he'll probably recognize me Christmas morning.

"I'll get the paperwork and bring it out here. The door is open."

"Are the keys in the ignition?"

"Keys?" The man laughs. "Those are so old-school."

"So is space."

"Those are actually surprisingly roomy."

"I could put that entire car in the front seat of my Ford truck."

The guy laughs again. "Well, you can't do that now, can you? That little car is gonna be your best friend."

"I have enough friends, thank you very much."

I look back and see Pervis staring out the windshield. I wave at him. I know that somewhere in this journey, there's gonna be a number one hit single.

Before leaving, I open the door to the SUV and feel the warmth rush out. I extend my hand to Pervis. For a second, his beady eyes behind the narrow glasses contemplate whether or not to even shake. Then he gives me a very weak grip.

"Thanks for all your help, man," I tell him.

I've already given him his money. I did that when I filled his tank of gas right before we arrived here.

"Don't get my cousin killed," Pervis says in a way that sounds like it doesn't really matter what happens to me. "Don't touch her, either."

I manage to get both of our suitcases wedged into the trunk of the micro car. I stack them on top of each other. Thankfully neither Cara nor I packed heavily. Most of my stuff is heading back to Nashville on the tour bus with the band.

"So, you ready?" I ask Cara.

"This is going to be an experience," she says.

Pervis turns toward her. "I still don't know why you even want to rush to be with that insane bunch."

"Someone needs to take care of them."

"That's just plain sad," Pervis says.

"Yes, it is." Cara leans over and kisses the guy on his cheek. "I'd say you're welcome to come, but we don't have room."

"Please. I've done my share of family outings with those nuts. No thanks."

"Thank you."

Before I shut the door, Pervis grins and gives me his prediction.

"You're never going to make it to Tulsa," he says. "Especially driving that thing."

I never knew exactly what your father told you that one day the two of you went out fishing. He came back and simply said, "I did it." When I asked what he did, he said he told you the truth. I assumed he was just encouraging you in your career, saying some doors shut and that's life. But the next day, you were headed back to Nashville with a renewed fire in your soul. Whatever he said obviously spoke to you.

I miss your father dearly. I'm sure you do too.

CHAPTER NINETEEN

Have Yourself a Merry Little Christmas

$\mathcal{T}$hick flakes the size of my fist fly by us like stars streaming past a rocket ship. Well, maybe not a rocket ship, but the jettison pod once the rocket ship has gone down. It's dark and we have Christmas music playing just to keep our spirits up. Just to help us not think about this little kiddie car we're in and the monstrous storm surrounding us. Cara shuffles in her seat a lot, unable to keep still.

"So what would you normally be doing right around now?" I ask after thinking about my family at home in Okmulgee.

"Cleaning up some kind of mess," Cara says.

"Yeah?" For some reason, I'm picturing a house full of kids. "What, from little ones running around?"

"No. From drunken idiots. The mess can be physical or

emotional. Always just depends on the mood and the wind and the way the night unfolds."

"Sounds like fun."

She doesn't say anything for a moment.

"I was joking."

"I wasn't," she says.

"Sorry."

"I usually am too by the end of Christmas."

I'm driving about forty miles an hour in what feels like a forty-inch car. For a moment, I remain silent.

"Total buzzkill," Cara says in a dronelike voice. "Sorry."

"Nah. I'm just wondering—so why the rush home, then? Like your cousin asked."

"Every game needs a referee."

"Maybe some games shouldn't be played."

"Yeah. But there's nothing I can do about that. You're born into the family you're born into without any say."

"So you're worried someone's setting the house on fire?"

"The house?" Cara is sitting facing me directly. "No—I'm afraid someone's gonna set someone else on fire."

"Maybe I better drive faster."

"I think I could run faster than this."

I look at her and then we start laughing. And we keep laughing. And it's just one of those I'm-so-dang-tired-and-look-at-us-now sort of laughs. It's a good kind, too, because I'm not two sheets to the wind, and I'm laughing at the utter lunacy of this.

"You're going to get home and tell your family you were with some crazy lady," Cara says, wiping the tears from her eyes. "Or, no—you're going to write a song out of this."

"A song? You kiddin' me? This is worthy of a whole Christmas album."

"Grandma didn't get run over by the reindeer. It was the pizza deliveryman."

"'Twas the night before Christmas, and all through the micro car. Not a muscle was stirring, until I let go with that micro fart."

"Flatulence jokes?" Cara says. "Have we really resorted to those?"

We make up songs like this for a few minutes, but we're so tired and slaphappy that it becomes hard to think of more. At least to think of more that are funny.

"So what would you be doing right now?" Cara asks.

"We've always opened one Christmas present on Christmas Eve. Always. My mother loved traditions and this was one. So they surely did this earlier with all my sisters and their husbands and the kids picking out one single gift to open."

"So what's your favorite Christmas memory?"

I think for a while but shrug. "I don't know."

"Oh, come on."

"I don't. Seriously. Sometimes—it's weird, but well, everything about our relationship has been weird, so I can just say it—but sometimes it feels like those times belonged to another kid. It belonged to another story I read about."

"You read about but don't even remember?" Cara says.

I nod. "You know—I do have a memory. I remember there was a large wrapped present—it was huge. From an uncle of mine. I couldn't wait to open it, so I opened it on Christmas Eve. Even though my parents suggested other presents. I tore off the wrapping paper and saw it was this vintage picture in a frame. It was a painting of a really cool bookcase full of old books. I hated the gift. Seriously. I was like, 'What is this?' Now it's one of my favorite possessions. Have it in my guest room in Nashville. It reminds me of my childhood."

"Bigger isn't always better," Cara says.

"Got that right. Just don't tell that to the people who work in the music business. They don't want big. They want huge."

A speed-limit sign says seventy-five miles an hour, which is about twice as fast as we're driving. This is ridiculous.

"So do you have one all-time-favorite memory?" I ask.

"I do. I remember—I was in ninth grade and my father wasn't around. That was the Christmas he bailed on the family. All the tension and the chaos weren't there. And I remember watching my brother opening his presents—he's a couple years younger than I am. I remember seeing him so happy. I remember laughing a lot. It's not that I got a pony for Christmas or anything like that. It's that—there really was a peace that year. It was a first. And a last."

"You still close with your brother?"

Cara nods and then looks away.

"But he stayed in New York."

"He might never come back to Oklahoma."

She says this in a way that someone might tell you their uncle just passed away.

"So you keep going to see him then," I say.

"My brother is slipping away the same way my father did when I was a teenager. He's in rehab. I did have an accounting conference I attended in New York, but I saw him right before I left the city. And he didn't look so good. That's why—when you first saw me—I was going out of my mind because I was thinking of him."

I want to say something, but I can feel this ten-pound car slipping even though I'm only going thirty miles an hour. The freeway is getting worse.

"So we've been in this car for half an hour already—"

"It's gonna take us probably ten hours to get to Tulsa," I say, completing her thought. "Even though it's a four-hour drive."

A small drift of snow is on the freeway and I plow into it, causing the car to slide sideways for a moment.

"Then again, we might not make it."

"Seriously?" Cara asks.

"Yeah, seriously. If it keeps comin' down like this. And if the roads keep lookin' like this. I haven't seen a plow for a while."

"At least we have a lot of room to stretch out in case we're snowbound."

"That's not even funny," I say.

My legs already are aching and my rear is numb.

So this is what happens. We keep driving and driving and driving. And it keeps snowing and snowing and snowing. And of course, we're just too stupid to pull off at one of the seven hundred exits and gas stations alongside the freeway. Nope. We just keep talking and laughing until boom—we're stuck in a ten-foot snowdrift. Snowbound and stuck. And you know what that means, right?

We gotta use body heat to keep ourselves warm. The phones won't work. We might die. We'll get frightened. Cara will need some TLC. I'll sing her a romantic song. She'll cuddle up beside me. Then sparks will fly and we'll welcome more snow to keep us in this wonderful winterland bliss.

Yeah, right.

No. Neither of us is that stupid. Sparks or not, being snow-bound on I-49 doesn't sound fun or romantic or entertaining.

Eventually, after driving another thirty minutes and going slower and slower, along with not seeing any snowplows or other vehicles out here, I decide to pull off at one of those massive trucker gas station all-inclusive-vacation hot spots. The all-in-one variety that has everything you can imagine. They're big enough to still be open on Christmas Eve. People are there because some people still have to work.

It's around eleven p.m. as I pull up beside the building.

"Mele Kalikimaka is the thing to say on a bright Hawaiian Christmas Day," I sing in my best Bing Crosby voice.

Cara bursts out in a laugh.

"*That* song is going on my Christmas album. I will refuse to do an album if I can't put that song on it."

"Nothing beats *Christmas Vacation*. Nothing."

"It's a tradition in our house too," I say.

"Imagine that family, except imagine a really angry, drunken Chevy Chase. That's my family."

"Tonight I'm your family," I tell her.

"Are you my boyfriend or my brother?"

"Aw, nah. You didn't just say that."

"I did."

"That's just plain wrong. Wrong."

"I love my brother," Cara says.

I shake my head. "So we might be stayin' here for quite a while. Sister."

She smiles and doesn't seem to mind. Strangely enough, I don't seem to mind either.

*　　*　　*

Cara comes around an aisle in the big supersaver mart we're in, wearing this big grin, as if she knows the secret route home. Her hair is no longer in a ponytail but rather loose and wavy, the blond reflecting the fluorescent lights like a halo around her face.

"What?"

"Okay—I have an idea," she says, biting her lip and looking like a teenager. "We're going to uphold the Sawyer tradition. We're going to give each other one present to open. How does that sound?"

For a moment she waits for me to respond. I'm currently holding a bottle of wine in one hand and a twelve-pack of beer in the other.

"Good heavens," Cara says, finally seeing the booze. "Where's the party and am I invited?"

"It might be a long night."

"Well, yeah, it might be now," she says, shaking her head. "I might be driving us home if the roads clear."

"It looks like Antarctica outside. We're not going anywhere."

"Okay. Well, before you go out barhopping, why don't you find me a present for our exchange?"

"Good idea," I say.

"Oh, and Heath—no alcohol. Got it?"

I nod.

Of course, she's only talking about herself.

I can't remember the last time I felt this young and silly and stupid. Especially when I wasn't completely soused. I spend the next hour wandering the aisles of this gas station with Cara, examining things I've never bothered to look at in my life. Like how many kinds of candy bars really do exist. Or how the choices are grouped—sweet here, salty there, healthy in this tiny section, double-sized bars over there. Or some of the strange items for sale, like underwear. Who runs into a gas station to buy a Coke and some Doritos and oh, yeah, throw in that pack of tidy whities?

There's a little section of audiobooks, and I contemplate getting her a scary-looking novel called *Marooned*, by Dennis Shore. There's a big bin of cheap CDs, and Cara browsing and laughing and telling me she can't wait to find one of my albums there. I tell her there will probably be quite a few. But so far, none can be spotted.

I see a trucker buying a hot dog with chili on it. Okay, I assume he's a trucker, but who knows? All I really know is this is a man brave enough to buy a hot dog that's probably been sitting there all day long, topped with some chili made out of God-only-knows what kind of meat. This is his Christmas Eve meal, something I point out to Cara, which she finds hilarious.

Cara tries to find a magazine that might have an article on me, but no luck. Fortunately.

She tells me to stay away while she buys my present, but I keep watching her and she keeps laughing and telling me to stay away. Suddenly we're both sixteen again and smiling and flirting and laughing and probably making the cashier think, *Get a room, you two.* And maybe if there was one nearby and available, maybe we would.

I see Cara brush her blond hair back and then smile and

say something to the cashier and suddenly I feel . . . weird. Like high-school-boy-crush weird.

Am I that tired and can't see that straight? Do I need a set of reality glasses on so I can see the accurate picture?

"Do you have your gift picked out?" she shouts.

I think so. I browse the aisles again and then tell her she can't look. I find the wine and beer I already purchased and then add the CD to it. I'm tempted to ask the cashier if he can gift wrap that, but he doesn't seem to be very cheery. Maybe I'll refrain.

"Oh, wait. Hold on. Buy this."

She makes me come to her so she won't see the gift I'm getting her. In her hand is a foot-tall Christmas tree. Fully decorated and playing "Have Yourself a Merry Little Christmas" as sung by Christina Aguilera.

"It matches our car," Cara says.

"Perfect."

As I buy these gifts, I have a sorta out-of-body experience.

I'm in a truck stop in the middle of Oklahoma (or are we still in Missouri?). I just purchased a Christmas gift (and still need to get some for my family). The nine months of touring seem like they belong to some other guy in some other life. Cara waits for me by the door, a grin on her face.

"Hurry it up," she calls out.

I wonder what it'd be like. The simple joy of staying with her. The simplicity of her life. The simple wealth of her vast soul.

Fame doesn't make you wiser or your soul richer. It only complicates the messy parts to begin with. Simplicity can be a glorious and beautiful thing. And to be honest, nobody is simple when you really start to get to know them. Nobody.

I open the door to the storm outside and we head to our car again.

Tonight, it will be our family room. We'll toast and open our presents and then listen to a Christmas tree sing to us. And I'm gonna love every single second of it.

Remember the year I gave you that picture of the guy in the rodeo? I wanted to give you something that would always remind you of Okmulgee. I put a note on the back that simply said, "Never Forget Your Home." I know it's not been easy, but you never have forgotten your roots. No matter how bright the lights become, this will still always be the place you belong.

CHAPTER TWENTY

Baby, It's Cold Outside

'm opening up a CD and am reminded that the best thing about digital downloads is they don't come with that sticky little strip that's fastened onto the sides of compact discs. I've been trying to get it off for a few minutes now.

"Let me try," Cara says. "I have longer fingernails."

"Maybe I'm not meant to open it."

"Yes, you are," she says.

The car is running and the heater is keeping us warm. The good thing is if we run out of gas, we can refuel without moving the car more than fifty feet. Snow covers the windows and I'm sorta glad. It gives us some privacy.

We both thought alike for our Christmas presents. I gave her one of the best country albums ever made. *Ever.* And I've spent the last half hour playing her my favorite songs off it. I tell her the gamble the artist took on it, and how the label thought the arrangements were too sparse and sounded like demos, but how the singer had complete creative control on it. Of course, *Red Headed Stranger* by Willie Nelson became a huge, huge success.

"Sometimes the people at the label don't know jack," I tell Cara.

"Maybe they just don't know his last name," she jokes.

We listen to several songs and then I open my gift. It's another CD, and another classic.

"Ever heard of this album?" she asked.

"No, never. *Bad*? Who would name an album *Bad*?"

I wonder why such a classic album, just like *Red Headed Stranger*, would be in a bargain bin.

"Well, they just released an anniversary edition of this," Cara says.

"I bet you got it."

"Downloaded it. I have everything by Michael Jackson."

"You know—if I died, my sales would quadruple."

"Do you want me to do you a favor?" she jokes.

I'm drinking wine out of a coffee mug I bought. Cara is refraining.

"Here—I'll play my favorite song off the album."

"I bet it's 'Dirty Diana.'"

"No, but I do love that song."

She plays me a slow song from the album, one I've never heard before.

"What's he saying?" I ask. "'Librarian Girl'?"

"'*Liberian* Girl.'"

"It's totally librarian girl. That's why you like it. You got that cute librarian-girl-next-door thing happening."

"Shut up. I like this song."

"'I love you, librarian girl,'" I copy.

"You're ruining the song."

"So wait—Liberia—is that a country?"

Cara shakes her head, takes my cup and sips from it. "You're such a redneck."

"I'm just wondering."

"Be quiet."

I mock sing the song. She nudges me. I study her face, so close up. She still amuses me.

"Librarian girl," I sing.

We listen to the album a little more, but then I tell her I want to put Willie back on. Cara turns the radio on instead, where a Burl Ives Christmas song is playing.

"So how do you write a song?" she asks as she takes the coffee mug from me and finishes off the wine.

"I thought you didn't want any?"

"I changed my mind," she says.

Her look is very telling. Gone is the woman I met at the airport who acted like I was her little brother who needed help. There's something there. And she's not even bothering to hide it.

"Women have a tendency to do that," she says. "We like to keep our options open."

"Oh, do you, librarian girl?"

I fill the cup again. Burl Ives is moaning through "Silver and Gold" and I can't take it anymore. I change the station to fit the mood. Thankfully, I find just the right woman for the job.

God bless you, Sade.

"So tell me," Cara says. "I want to learn from the best."

"Oh, gonna try to write a song?"

Her sweater fits her snug, like fancy gift wrap around a present I can't wait to open. The scarf wrapped around her neck is dangling like a bow ready to be pulled. Suddenly I love this tiny car and how close the seats are and the fact that there's not some massive barricade between us.

"I always start with a beat," I tell her.

"A beat, huh? You don't start plucking at the guitar?"

I shake my head and don't take my eyes off of her.

"It always depends on what I'm writing about."

"Write a song now," Cara tells me.

"It'd be a slow ballad."

"Really?"

I put the coffee cup down and then I change the radio. I find a country station and hear a beautiful song by a beautiful woman singing about the Oklahoma sky.

"This fits you," I say. "Songs do that, you know? Some fit you like a pair of your favorite jeans or that denim jacket you love."

"I like this song," Cara says. "So keep going."

"I'd write some lyrics about the cold outside and the warmth in this car."

I take her hands without thought. For a moment, I just feel them. They're strong and soft and long.

"I'd talk about the bad weather and then about your beauty," I say.

"I think you've had too much to drink."

"I haven't even started."

"You could call your song 'I Finally Lost It on Christmas Eve.'"

"Maybe you're right," I tell her, moving closer to her.

She isn't moving away, isn't pulling her hands away. She still wears that look. The wanting, needing look. The safe look. The sweet, innocent look.

"I didn't realize I'd make it home tonight," I say to her comforting smile.

The singer on the radio says she's homeward bound, and that's when I kiss Cara. Everything about the kiss is just like her look. It's safe and sweet and reminds me of the feeling I've had on this night many times in the past. A feeling of security and warmth.

The song trails off and Cara pulls away from me. She still holds my hands.

"So are you my guardian angel?" I ask her with a grin.

"No. But I could be your accountant."

I laugh. "That's, like, the sexiest thing I've ever heard someone say."

Cara smiles. "That's me. Totally sexy."

I'm about to answer this with another kiss when suddenly a loud knock sounds on the window behind Cara. Both of us jerk like a pair of teenagers caught messing around in the driveway. She pulls away and then opens the window.

"Hey—you guys okay?" It's a guy in a winter cap and a thick winter coat. "You stranded here?"

I let out a sigh.

We were doing just fine before you showed up.

"Yeah, we're a bit stranded," Cara says.

No, we're not. Please just go away.

This nice intimate moment and the sanctuary of our tiny car are gone.

"Everything okay?" the man asks.

"Besides our flight canceling and our train crashing, yeah, everything's okay," I tell him.

"You're Heath Sawyer."

"Yes, sir," I say.

"Wow," he says, looking at the interior of the micro car in disbelief.

"This is the *only* way I roll," I joke.

"Wait till my wife hears about this. Hey—do you guys need a place to stay?"

Cara looks back at me, knowing what I'm thinking but also realizing the situation.

"Yeah, I think we do," I tell the kind-faced stranger.

You have to take the good with the bad. This is what life is all about. One of the best years of my life was when you finally got your record deal. It would also be one of the worst, since that was when your father first discovered the cancer that would eventually kill him. You gotta be thankful for each day we're given and for each blessing bestowed on us. Then you gotta make the most of them.

CHAPTER TWENTY-ONE

Let It Snow, Let It Snow, Let It Snow

*W*e have more room in the large cab of this Chevy truck than we had in the micro car we left behind moments ago. Cara sits in the middle as we steadily make our way down the interstate. The driver is Nathan Birdwell, an easygoing thirty-something guy who reminds me of some of my buddies back home. A good ol' Oklahoman helping out some stranded strangers. Granted, one of them happens to be pretty famous, but that's okay. I want to believe he'd do this for most anybody.

After a few minutes in the truck, he asks the inevitable question.

"So what's a guy like you doing stranded out here on Christmas Eve? Is this going to make the tabloids or something?"

"Last-minute plans," I tell him. "Didn't realize the weather was out to get me."

"Oklahoma weather," Nathan says, sounding as tired as I feel. "Been a bad year for us Okies."

"We're resilient," I say. "Even if some of us get stranded at gas stations."

I nudge Cara's side.

"My wife loves you. If she wasn't already asleep, I think she'd flip out knowing I was bringing you home."

"Thank you so much for your hospitality," Cara says.

"That really was a tiny car," Nathan says. "Say—don't you celebrity types usually travel with entourages and all that?"

"Sometimes," I say. "I didn't want all that extra baggage."

"Good thing the two of you are together."

Neither of us says anything. I elbow Cara, hoping she finds the humor in his statement.

We're riding down I-44 in his truck with a snowplow that's clearing the road in front of us. It's not too bad, but the wind is furious and every now and then there comes a large drift that we crash through.

"They have the big state plows doing the interstate, but I figure why not help 'em out a bit?"

"Bad night to have to plow, huh?" I ask.

"I'm actually glad, to be honest. I'm a teacher at a private school, but since my wife is a full-time mother to our three little ones, I have to pick up money whenever I can. Last winter was pretty tough in terms of plowing. There wasn't a lot of snow, so there wasn't much work."

This amiable guy with a family of four back home *wants* to

be out tonight, on Christmas Eve, plowing the roads and being away from his family.

"How old are your children?" Cara asks.

"We have a six-year-old daughter and then twin two-year-olds. All girls."

"Dang. I hope you have a set of shotguns at your home," I tell him.

Nathan laughs. "I'm saving up for them."

Cara and Nathan talk for a while about the girls and it's cute and I can tell Nathan loves them dearly, but I can't relate. They might as well be talking about trigonometry.

"One of the girls got pretty sick this winter. Had to be in the hospital a couple of times after getting pneumonia. The twins were preemies and the smaller of the two has always been less healthy."

"Sorry to hear that," I tell him.

"It's just called being a parent."

"I hope staying with you isn't any sort of inconvenience?"

"No, not at all. I welcome other males. Sometimes I open my eyes and all I see is pink."

"I'd like to give you some kind of encouragement," I tell him. "But, buddy—I'll tell you straight. You're in trouble. *Big* trouble."

Nathan has a casual, slow laugh. "Yeah, I know. If I had a buck for everybody who tells me, 'Wait until they're teenagers,' I'd be rich."

"That's not very nice," Cara says. "Who's to say they'll be troublemakers?"

"Oh, they'll be troublemakers," I say, trying to be funny.

"Ignore him," Cara says to Nathan. "He's just trying to be witty."

"A week ago we thought Brittany might take a turn for the worse, the way everything looked. We brought her back home from the hospital the first time but then had to take her back. She was so weak. Thankfully she got better. Since then I've been reminded that all I can do is try to provide for these little ladies and get on my knees and ask God to take care of them. The rest—well, yeah, they're already troublemakers. They take after their father."

I can't find anything witty to say about that, so I stay quiet. The world outside is speckled and streaking across the windshield. We can only see a short distance with the headlights.

"I think the snow's gonna stop in the middle of the night," Nathan says. "I'm gonna be plowing, but it's supposed to get better. I can gladly take y'all back to the station to get your car whenever you want tomorrow."

"You're a kind soul in a snowstorm," I tell him.

"I'd hope you'd do the same for me."

I think about that statement for a moment and am not sure if I would. I'd like to say I would, but would I really, truly stop and really, truly allow myself to help a complete stranger out in the middle of the night?

No.

We turn at an exit and head into the darkness. I don't say anything more. Instead, I think of what he said. The words replay over and over again in my head.

I hope you'd do the same for me.

I don't know.

I know it's Christmas and of course I say I'd do anything

and maybe I would. But lately, it just seems like I've been so busy and so determined and so single-minded that I might literally overlook thinking about helping another stranded soul.

My eyes close for a second.

I think I'm really tired, even if I can't stop and admit it.

I think I could close my eyes for a year and be okay with it.

Maybe that's what I'll do when I get home. Take a little break that lasts God only knows how long.

Yeah, right, Heath.

The house is a modest two-story in a small neighborhood. Everything is smothered with snow, so I don't see much in the midnight dark. We enter through the open garage and find the house completely quiet.

"There's a guest room downstairs," he says. "We're one of the few houses around with a basement. It's fixed up—has a bath and everything. Y'all will be fine down there."

Again, Cara and I don't say anything as we carry our bags down the carpeted stairs and to the bedroom with the queen-sized bed. Nathan gives me his cell phone and tells me to call him if something comes up.

"I texted my wife that I have a couple staying with us, but she sometimes doesn't check texts, so I'm gonna tell her y'all are here before I head out again. I'll probably be out a few more hours."

"I'm sorry," Cara says.

"I'm not. It's work. Pays pretty good, too."

We thank him and then hear him head back upstairs. Then

we both look at the bed, then back at each other. Cara's eyes say, *Don't even think about it.*

"What?" I ask her.

"I want you to know—I'm a good girl."

"Okay." I reply in a way that makes it seem like I have no idea what she's talking about.

"I know what you're thinking and don't even try to play any games with me."

"I didn't want anything to be awkward," I say. "That's all."

"So why do you have a not-so-good look on your face?"

"So why are you smiling?"

"Inside I'm screaming," Cara says.

"You gotta admit. That was a nice kiss back there."

"You only get to open *one* present on Christmas Eve."

I laugh. "You know—you're not like any accountant I've ever met."

"Meet a lot of accountants in your line of work?"

"No."

"Okay, then."

I examine the room. "Okay, listen. I'll sleep on the floor. They can go ahead and think we're a couple, and when he writes the tell-all story to the gossip magazines, you'll have to deny everything."

"Nathan looks like he can keep a secret."

"Well, we haven't met the missus, have we?" I say. "They get to you in every way they can. It gets old, to be honest. You start to grow wary about everyone."

"So why weren't you wary of me?"

"You didn't even know who I was," I tell her. "You're just— you seem trustworthy."

"What if I really was a reporter instead of an accountant trying to get home?"

I take a pillow off the bed and shrug. "There's nothing I've done that I haven't done for the last decade. There's already plenty of dirt on me for people to see. If you were a reporter, you could share how much of a gentleman I was on Christmas Eve."

"The night's not over," Cara says in a playful way.

"Now don't you go starting that sorta talk. *That* is what messes with men's heads. Just so you know."

Cara leaves to use the restroom and I check my phone. I've sorta been ignoring it tonight and I see the result. I have twenty texts and all sorts of e-mails and notifications.

Right now I'm too tired to pay attention to any of this. Nothing looks too urgent. The world goes on hold around Christmastime. Which is really fine by me, because I need someone to tell me to go on hold.

I just need a really bad storm and a really nice accountant.

Cara comes back into the room dressed in sweatpants and a matching sweatshirt.

"Man, nothing tempts me more than a good sweat suit," I say, and get swatted on the arm.

I go to brush my teeth and then to find a blanket.

Maybe a cold shower would be good too.

When someone asks me to name your greatest talent, I tell them it's the ability to wait. It's the incredible patience. The persistence and the refusal to give up. Those years you had to wait before your first album came out, before your first single was released—those were the years that impressed me. Again, it would be so easy for most people to simply give up. But you once said you couldn't give up. Country music was a part of you just like your heart and your lungs. Country music is your soul.

CHAPTER TWENTY-TWO

O Holy Night

$\mathscr{I}$ hear Cara's voice speaking in the darkness. But it's not in either of my dreams, my literal one or my imagined one. The voice is coming from up above me, like an angel speaking out to a poor helpless man.

"How's it going down there?"

"This is what I dreamt about when I was younger," I say. "Getting the girl, sleeping on the floor next to her bed."

"Shut up."

I'm right next to the bed, with a blanket covering me and a malnourished pillow not really doing its job.

"I'm fine. Thanks for asking. I can't feel anything below my waist. I'll never perform on a stage again. So really—thank you."

There's a pause in the darkness; then I hear her laughing.

"What?" I ask.

"I could say a lot, but I won't. This isn't the time for innuendos."

"Haven't I already showed you how harmless I am?"

"You're not the only one in this room I'm worried about."

For a second I wonder who else she's talking about.

Oh, yeah. Ah, got it.

Turning out the lights had been slightly awkward, even with my attempts at making everything comical. I didn't know what to say and neither did she, and then we both said, "Good night," at the same time, and then we both stopped in mid-sentence. Then I just cursed and turned out the light.

"I know you think I'm a prude," Cara says.

"I never said that."

"I know you're thinking that."

"Maybe I was thinking of my mother's pies."

"You were?"

I shake my head in the darkness. "No."

For a while she doesn't say anything. But I know she's not sleeping. I know she's not even trying to sleep. I can just hear the motors to her brain working.

"I'll just tell you now this isn't going to work out. You and I. You know that, right?"

"I'm sleeping on the floor," I say, again. "What part of to-night makes you think I believe *anything* is working out?"

I hear her shuffle in the bed to face me. "Maybe this is the chivalrous act to suck me in."

"Is it working?"

"Absolutely," she says, then pauses, then adds, "Not."

"That kiss was nice."

"Yes, it was."

"That's a kiss you can build something off of," I say.

"No. You can't. We can't, because the guy kissing is this guy named Heath Sawyer. Big-time country star that makes all the girls swoon."

"There was a time people didn't know who that was. And even now I meet women in the restrooms who don't know who I am."

"Doesn't change who you are."

I sit up and lean over on the bed. "It's really not that—"

"Get back down," Cara orders.

"Dogs get treated better than this."

My head goes back against the pillow. I know I could fall asleep in a matter of seconds, if I really wanted to.

"So why are you in such a rush to get back home anyway?" she asks me.

"I'm not. I'm just—I guess if I was being honest, I'd say I'm rushing to keep up with you."

"But why even make the trip in the first place?"

"For my family," I say, staring at the ceiling that I can only imagine in the darkness along with other things. "Specifically, my mother. It's the first Christmas since my father passed away."

"So you're, like, the family rock too, huh?"

"Me? Nah. I'm like the court jester. The comic relief. No— it's just, they'll want me home. My mother and my sisters. I haven't been home since the funeral half a year ago."

"Have you been avoiding going back?"

"I've been on tour. I had a bit role in a movie. I'm supposed to be working on a follow-up album, not to mention a Christmas album too. Life's been busy."

"You've been avoiding going back home."

"Yeah," I admit.

Once again I feel like Cara has known me for a long time.

"I'm sure they're proud of you," she says.

"Sometimes. Unless I make a fool of myself for some reason."

"Like sleeping with a strange woman on Christmas Eve."

"You might be a lot of things, but you're not a strange woman," I say. "I've been with a few of those. You're like family."

"Oh."

She says this in a wounded sort of way.

Now is the time you sit up and slip in beside her and tell her what you really mean.

I don't think so.

She's already admitted she's attracted to you, and that kiss proved it, so why are you being such a wimp and sleeping on the floor?

It's the weirdest thing.

I'm not exactly sure why.

I've never been considered shy, especially when it comes to the ladies. But being here and being with Cara and being Christmas Eve and being everything all mean I'm stuck here on the floor.

I start to say something, then stop, then think of something else, then force myself to remain silent. If Cara wants to talk, let her talk.

And if she wants to smother me with all her accountant love, then let her do that as well.

So I wait. And I wait.

*   *   *

My eyes are closed and I swear I'm dreaming when I hear her call my name.

"Heath?"

"Yeah," I mumble.

"Are you awake?"

"No."

"I don't want to go home," Cara says.

"I don't think this family's going to want us staying with them."

Another pause, and once again I'm drifting off.

"Heath?"

"I'm still asleep," I joke.

"Merry Christmas."

"It certainly has been, hasn't it? Merry?"

Sometime later, I am in fact sleeping, and I imagine her calling out my name. Maybe just to see if I'm still awake. Or maybe it's just in my dreams. I don't know. But her voice is so close and I like hearing my name uttered by her in the middle of the night.

It just feels right.

We all thought it would happen with Reilly. I remember after you two called it quits, you told me, "Something in her's broken, Momma." I never told you what I maybe should've said at the time. We're all broken. Sometimes it's just a little more obvious in people. But we're all the same. Pieces that need mending. That's what marriage can do. It puts those pieces back together again.

CHAPTER TWENTY-THREE

Silver and Gold

*S*he's gone. Just like that.

I wake up with half of my body numb and a block of wood wedged in the back of my neck. It takes me a while to stand, but when I do, I notice the covers on the bed smooth and pulled back. Sunlight streaks in through the window. I check my phone, but the battery is dead.

When I go upstairs, I start hearing them. A couple. Arguing. No, not arguing, but screaming at each other.

"All I do is work my butt off and this is the kind of thanks I get, right?"

Nathan's yelling at someone. I'm thinking it's his wife.

"*You* try takin' care of three spoiled little brats all on your own! We never should've have moved to this godforsaken state—we should have stayed in L.A."

L.A.?

Something feels off. I'm beginning to think I need to go back downstairs, but then I hear the crying. I look back and see the twin girls sitting at the bottom of the stairs, gawking at me in terror and wailing in their elf pajamas.

"No, no—shh—come on," I begin to say, but it's too late.

I start to head downstairs but look up and suddenly see the largest woman I've ever seen in my life standing at the top of stairs. In a nightgown that resembles a tent. She's wearing Santa's cap and she's holding—

She's holding a knife. The kind you use to cut deer meat with.

The knife looks wet. It looks like it's dripping—

That's blood.

The girls keep crying and the woman at the top of the stairs starts laughing and then I hear her say down to me, " 'Redneck Reject' is my all-time favorite hit, so come here, big boy, and show me what you got."

I cough and jerk and feel half my body numb. But this time the sensation is real and not some crazy dream. The room is still dark and it's early morning. I don't hear anything. I wait for a while and hear a mild shuffling in the bed.

Okay, note to self: Never eat hot dogs from a gas station late at night like you did before getting in the truck with Nathan.

I sigh and wonder if I'm going to make it home today. This has been a real trip, but I'm ready for something normal. Well, my family has never been considered normal; I guess I should say something familiar.

Cara's familiar and you've only known her a couple of days.

I wonder how much longer I'll be able to say I know her. I wonder where we'll leave things once I finally officially say good-bye.

Maybe, possibly, it will be later today.

You didn't say hopefully.

"Dat my baby, Bitty."

The voice upstairs is loud and obviously belongs to one of the toddlers.

"It *my* baby."

The other voice responding is lower and sounds distinctly different.

"You go there and I go here."

"It *my baby,* Acin."

I've just taken a quick shower and am now hearing them outside the bathroom. I inch the door open and take a peek. Two blond-haired girls are sitting there, with several babies surrounding them. They keep talking, and it cracks me up. A television is on in the room. I see talking pastries, then something that says "Dandee Donuts."

Kids' shows. A universe I know nothing about.

Soon I hear steps and I know someone's coming. I decide I might as well say good morning to whoever shows up. The figure walking into the play area in the basement is a tall and attractive woman wearing dress pants and a vest with a dress shirt underneath. She looks like she's ready to go out shopping instead of dealing with these two toddlers in matching pajamas.

"Good morning," I tell her, trying not to freak her out. "I'm Heath."

"Hi, yes, I know. Such a pleasure to meet you. I'm Erin. Nathan's wife. He's upstairs."

We shake hands and I can see her face turn a bright pink.

"These are Brittany and Megan. Their nicknames are Itty and Acin. Their big sister, Kate, is upstairs. Hiding from you."

"Ah. Well, I'll have to find her. The twins are beautiful. I definitely see the difference."

"Yeah, especially now with the hair. Britt's hair is just like mine—straight and white-blond—while Megan's is more like her father's. Wavy and not as blond."

"Bet you have your hands full."

The woman smiles and nods. She resembles her husband—a friendly sort of soul who doesn't seem that surprised to have strangers in her basement on Christmas morning.

"Good morning," a voice calls out behind me.

Cara comes out of the bedroom all made up and looking a little like a wrapped Christmas present in silver and gold. I take her in and can't help grinning as the two women introduce themselves.

"I'm the designated driver of the trip," Cara jokes.

"Very funny," I say.

"We met in New York, believe it or not."

Erin tries to make sense of this. "So you guys aren't—"

"No, we're not a couple," Cara says.

"She likes to say that, but really she's my wife. We're just not telling anybody about it."

Erin laughs. I guess she knows my sense of humor from all my crazy songs.

"I'm sorry then, for putting you in one room—my husband thought—"

"It's fine, really," I say. "I slept on the floor."

I rub my neck and then get on my knees to play with the girls. They look at me with suspicious eyes.

We heard who you are and we aren't impressed, their eyes say.

One has bold and bright blue eyes and the other has more narrow, darker eyes. I can see the resemblance, but I'm captivated by noticing their differences.

"Their daddy has taught them to be wary of men," Erin says.

"I'm sure especially men like this one," Cara adds.

It's fun to see her interact with the girls. She's a natural. If this had been Naomi, she would have put on a doctor's mask and some plastic gloves and then stood there frozen.

Soon the eldest Birdwell daughter comes down to join us in the basement. She's tall for her age and has beautiful strawberry blond hair.

"I saw you on TV," six-year-old Kate tells me.

"Uh-oh," I say. "What was I doing?"

"You were singing."

"I was? Did I sound any good?"

"Well, kinda."

I laugh. "Well, that's a lot better than what some people say."

I smell bacon cooking upstairs and feel my stomach rumbling.

"I hope you guys aren't going to any trouble for us," I say to Erin.

"Nathan enjoys cooking, so it's no problem. Hope you don't mind a little breakfast?"

"I'm starving," I say.

"That would be wonderful, thank you," says Cara.

"It might be a little chaotic," Erin says.

"That's been the story of the last two days," I say. "And the last decade."

There's a moment in the middle of the breakfast where I suddenly leave the table I'm sitting at, surrounded by food and funny Christmas memories, and I just hover above it. Watching in wonder.

It's listening to a six-year-old describe what she can't wait to do later today. She says this in the way I've heard other kids talk about it many times before, the anticipation of waking up and finding presents by the tree and opening them. Except, in this case, it's not about opening presents but about giving them.

"We bring presents to poor people and then make them dinner," Kate says with a smile.

"It's with our church," Nathan says. "We like to say 'people who don't have as much as we do,' right, Kate?"

"Yeah."

"Yeah," one of the twins repeats.

I'm no longer eating my pancakes and bacon and eggs and drinking my coffee. I'm a spectator suddenly invited into a small family's heart and soul. A part of me feels like I shouldn't be here. But then again, I'm sitting next to Cara, and she feels right at home in the Birdwell household. While I'm watching everybody, that also includes Cara.

Can a guy like me really end up with a woman like her?

She talks to Brittany about Elmo and opens her mouth

wide and gets a big laugh from the girl, whose mouth is full of chocolate-chip pancakes.

Can someone who has ventured so far away from a family like this ever expect to have one like this in the future?

Cara nudges me and tries to get me to laugh at something she says.

Can a guy so focused on one thing and one thing only ever let go and laugh and live life a little?

"He's just tired from not flying in first class," Cara teases.

"I am," I say, coming back to reality. "I'm used to people helping me out instead of doing everything *opposite* of what I say."

"Do you like her?" Kate asks.

"Katie, no," Erin says, quickly apologizing.

"I do," I say to the young girl. "I'm totally smitten."

"Stop it," Cara says.

"Smitten?" Kate asks.

"Yeah. That means—that's sorta when you get something like poison ivy or something like that."

"Ewwww!"

Kate laughs and this makes the twins laugh too.

"That's me," Cara says. "A bad case of poison ivy."

I scratch behind my ears for effect. "It's going to be tough to get rid of this."

"He's gonna be scratching a long time."

Nathan and Erin are loving this. And you know what? So am I.

An hour later, before we go, I tell each of the girls I have a little Christmas present for them. Nathan and Erin both look surprised, acting like I'm doing something big.

"You guys let some strangers stay overnight with you," I remind them.

"Famous strangers," Erin says.

"I know—I get that all the time," Cara says while standing next to the large Christmas tree in the corner of the family room. "You might want to monitor the presents he gives. I don't think travel-sized vodka bottles are really for kids."

"Very funny," I say.

For the twins, I give each of them an iPhone cover. Someone gave me half a dozen of them for samples.

"Don't you think they're a little young for phones yet?" Cara asks.

Brittany takes her cover and sprints away as if she's afraid someone will take it from her. Megan starts biting hers.

"Yes, I know. But it's something."

"I often say we could give them coal and they'd play with it," Nathan says. "As long as we give them each a piece."

I haven't forgotten the big sister. "Here—this might be a little big for you, but you can grow into it."

It's a tour T-shirt. She unfolds it and I see the familiar picture of myself, the same smirk I have on the cover. It reads LIVING ON THE EDGE WITH HEATH SAWYER.

"It was either this or a 'Redneck Reject' shirt."

The parents are both happy and proud. The gifts might as well be for Nathan and Erin.

Since Nathan is going to take us back to the car, we say good-bye to Erin and the girls.

"Appreciate you guys helping us out," I say. "You all will have to come to my next show in Oklahoma."

Cara gushes and hugs Erin and says good-bye to the girls.

The snow has stopped falling and we can actually see the sun. I breathe the cold morning air and feel like we really might make it home today.

I can't remember the last time I wanted to get home so badly. It's a pretty cool feeling to have.

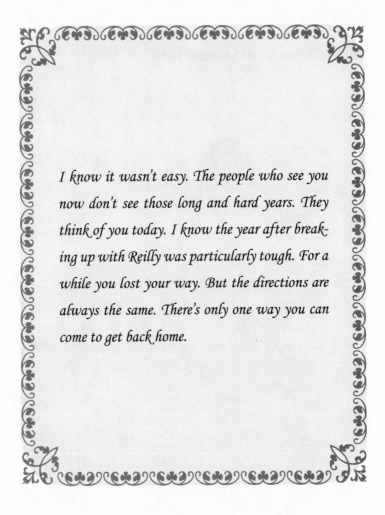

I know it wasn't easy. The people who see you now don't see those long and hard years. They think of you today. I know the year after breaking up with Reilly was particularly tough. For a while you lost your way. But the directions are always the same. There's only one way you can come to get back home.

CHAPTER TWENTY-FOUR

Please Come Home
for Christmas

ara punches my arm the moment we climb back into the micro car. "Was that not the cutest family you've ever seen?"

"They were pretty stinkin' adorable."

"Did you see all the presents under the tree? And did you hear how they're going to help make dinner for people in need?"

"I actually started to feel a little guilty hearing that," I say.

"You did?"

"Nah, not really," I joke.

"I'm just—I'm so bummed."

"For leaving?"

Cara shakes her head. "No. I'm bummed for having to go home. After seeing that. It's like riding a horse on a farm, then having to go scoop up manure right afterward."

I glance at her and she's not even trying to be funny or ironic. "You just compared going back to your home to scooping up manure."

"That's right."

"That's harsh. I'd hate to ever cross you."

Cara doesn't reply and I'm not sure what she's thinking, since I can't see her eyes behind her sunglasses. For a while we ride in silence. The interstate ahead of us looks plowed and clear. We're flying at seventy-five miles an hour. I turn on the radio and a guy sings about paper angels.

It takes ten minutes to realize that Cara's crying. Just my luck to make another woman cry without even knowing what I said.

"Hey—Cara—what's wrong?"

She shakes her head while I turn off the radio.

"What'd I say?"

"It's nothing," she says. "It's not you. It's me."

"What is it?"

"I know that sounded harsh and I don't mean to be harsh."

"I know. I was just teasin'."

"No, you were being honest and you're right. That's really awful of me to say that about my family. Especially on Christmas Day."

"Look, we all have dysfunctional families."

"Some people have dysfunctional families. Mine is more than that. Mine is deadly. It's like a poison and I have to be there so nobody ends up getting hurt or killed."

She's dead serious when she says this.

"Is it that bad?"

Cara nods, wiping her cheeks. "I hate being all girlie. I'm sorry."

"I have three sisters," I remind her.

She laughs for a moment. "Are they as hormonal and out of it as I am?"

"That's my description of every woman I've ever met. 'Course, I can't get away with saying that."

"When I was younger, I used to dream of that back there in Nathan's house. The family of five. Little girls running around making noise and laughing and screaming."

"So why hasn't it happened? You never met a Mr. Right?"

For a while Cara just looks out the front windshield at the surrounding countryside. "You have to actually get out of your house to meet a Mr. Right."

"There are online options, you know."

She crinkles up her nose at my joke.

"My last boyfriend told me I was too scared—too scared and too helpless—to cut the cord. He basically gave me an ultimatum, and I chose my family. Not because they were the better choice. But it's just . . ."

"They're your family," I say, understanding everything she's saying.

"You know—my brother, the one I was visiting. He's like this total and complete mess. And he has the gall to blame his problems on me."

"What?"

She nods. "Yeah. 'Cause I pushed him to get out and do something with his life. He said I pushed him away, but really I just wanted him away from the family so he could try to be his own self. But he's just a younger version of our father."

"So let me get this straight—you're the caretaker of the family and you try to get your younger brother to get away from them and yet he blames you now for him being a loser."

"He's not a loser," Cara snaps back.

"Okay."

"No, I take that back. He is a loser. A big-time loser. But you don't know him, so you can't say that about him."

"Come home with me," I blurt out.

I don't know where it came from and what it means, but there. I said it.

"What?"

"Come back home with me. Meet my momma and my sisters."

"Are you—are you serious?"

"Totally," I say.

She shakes her head and her hair drifts in front of her face. "How can you be serious?"

"You take a break from being your family's guardian angel and whipping girl."

"It's Christmas," she says, as if to remind me.

"I know. And shouldn't you get a break?"

"No. No way. That's crazy."

I see a sign for Tulsa that says it's forty-five miles away.

"You know," I say, "you never know when Mr. Right might be *right* in front of you. Or maybe beside you, driving a really hot micro car."

"You say that now, but that's just because you're tired from being on tour and you probably haven't spent a lot of time with normal people in a while."

"You're normal?" I joke.

"When you get home you'll think I was some cute and amusing girl you met and spent some time with, but seriously— what more are you going to think?"

"You're pretty hard on yourself."

Cara nods. "You should see my father."

"Yeah, maybe I should. I could tell him a thing or two about life."

"He's seen and heard it all before. We've had three interventions for this man. He's as stubborn as a mule. Or even more stubborn."

"So then come home—"

"Heath? No. End of subject. Thanks, but no. Okay?"

I raise my eyebrows and sigh and then nod.

"I was in such a great mood and now I'm falling into an abyss," Cara says. "Can we just stop talking about it and maybe think about Christmas?"

"Of course."

"Can I turn the radio back on?"

"Crank 'er up."

She goes to find a station. "I want some Christmas music to put me in the spirit."

"I want some spirits to do that," I joke.

Well, actually I'm not joking.

I need a big stiff drink. And then a few more.

"There," Cara says, finding a Christmas song. "That's more like it."

The song changes, and suddenly Judy Garland is telling us to have a merry little Christmas. Her voice is so distinct and beautiful, but it sounds so sad. So fragile. The song always seems to be like someone saying, *Look, try to suck it up because life's hard and I know and I might actually cry right now.*

I try to hide my smile. Cara looks out her window and I know this can't be cheering her up.

"Until then, we'll have to muddle through somehow."

Yeah, that just puts me in such a festive mood.

Next up, the radio plays another similar song. It's the unmistakable Eagles singing a tale of loss in "Please Come Home for Christmas." I look at Cara and she tries to squelch her smile.

"Really?" she asks.

"It's a classic," I tell her.

"Did the DJ just break up with his childhood sweetheart or something? I mean, come on."

This is a song I'd love to cover on a Christmas album. I haven't heard it for a while. It's complete with a small guitar solo.

The third song that comes on is another classic, and another familiar Christmas song: Elvis singing about having a "Blue Christmas."

"That's it. Enough."

Cara turns the radio off and I think if she could, she would rip it out and leave it on the side of the Oklahoma highway.

"There are happy Christmas songs. They don't all have to be sad."

"It's a sign," I joke.

"Yeah, that the DJ went off her meds. Come on."

She's the one who starts it. Soon she's laughing; then I'm laughing too. Then we're laughing and I'm not sure exactly what we're laughing about. But I love it. Cara has tears running down her cheeks.

"I think *I'm* the one who needs meds," she says.

"My doctor prescribes Jim Beam."

When we stop laughing, I tell her I'll find us a good song. A good country song. I find a familiar station.

"This station is great. Been on here many times. Of course, you wouldn't know that, would you?"

A Christmas song sung by Carrie Underwood comes on.

"See, this is upbeat and fun. Just like country music should be."

Just like your Christmas could be if you listened to me.

We're not far from Tulsa and from me saying good-bye to Cara. We've been riding in silence. I can't help but think about my momma and my sisters and getting home to them. It's gonna feel good to be back at the old house and just relax. Just be myself, the Heath Sawyer they've seen for thirty-five years, and not try to be or do anything more.

A country song comes on that's not a Christmas song but just a song.

Just another song. Like just another passenger in a car, or just another Christmas morning, or just another girl, or just another smile.

No such thing as just another anything.

The song plays and I drive and I occasionally look over at a face that's trying not to look at me. The landscape suddenly loses its color and the white of the snow suddenly seems dim because all I'm doing is thinking of her. A good song—heck, a great song—will do that to you. Transport you even when you're moving at seventy miles an hour. Move you even when you're making your way slowly back home. Prompt you even when you've been stuck for so long.

"Stop it," Cara says.

"What?"

"You know what."

She smiles back at me. This is a moment and we both know it. The song serves to remind us. I can tell she feels the same thing I do.

"I thought you didn't like country," I say.

"I have a pulse, don't I?"

I shrug and feel her fist in my shoulder.

Maybe I've been on the road too long and I need to stabilize my sanity when I'm back home. I don't know. All I know is I like that grin. Trouble. Complex. Cute but with so much underneath. Cute and sexy but not an overt sexy but just a cute.

You've lost your mind.

Maybe I don't care if I have. Maybe I'm slowly becoming myself again the closer to home I'm getting. The Oklahoma air is soaking into my skin and I'm suddenly able to breathe again and suddenly able to see again and I can see something I really, truly think is a beautiful thing. This friend and this figure next to me. Listening to the song and letting her eyes linger and maybe—possibly—hopefully—loving it just a little.

"Nice song," she finally says when it's over.

It's a nice moment, the kind that happens so seldom in this busy, loud, brash world.

When all that trouble happened in L.A. with the reporter you knocked out (and you know, to this day I'm proud you socked him), I knew you needed to get away. It was nice having you hide out and do things you spent your youth loving to do. Hunting. Fishing. Spending time outdoors. All the concert halls in the world will never compete with the calm of an Oklahoma countryside.

CHAPTER TWENTY-FIVE

Same Old Lang Syne

*T*guide the car through familiar streets in Tulsa and then toward a friendly subdivision. We're soon outside a modest one-story single-family home.

A single-family home for a single soul.

"I made it," Cara says.

"You made it."

"Thanks to you."

"Thanks to both of us."

"Nice little place, huh?"

I nod and look out the window. A lot of thoughts go through my mind. Now isn't the time to be witty or elusive. Now is the time to be as honest as I possibly can be.

"I'd like to see you again," I say.

"Really? Okay, well, let's just for a moment assume that's true."

"Why wouldn't it be?"

"That's what you tell all the girls you're stranded and stuck with in strangers' houses."

"Yeah, every single one," I say.

"So what—so you see me again. In real life and real time."

"And that would be bad?"

"Some things—some situations—some people are just not meant to be together."

"Is there some rule book you're quoting there?"

"The 'How to Keep Yourself from Being Completely Miserable Book.'"

"This trip hasn't been miserable."

"No, but I bet real life sure would be. I don't want a guy who spends nine months on the road."

"Nothing says you can't join me," I say.

Maybe it's a bit much to say. She hasn't even said yes to a date and here I am inferring that she'd go on tour with me.

"I'm just sayin'—," I start to say.

"This is not—*I'm* not some kind of country song."

"I can cover Michael Jackson if you want me to."

"But that's it. That's the thing. I don't want to be a cover song. I want to be an original. With maybe a Linn LM-1 drum machine playing in the background."

"Prince reference," I say. "Impressive."

She looks surprised.

"I might sing about being a redneck, but that doesn't mean I don't know music. I know the stuff I need to know."

"Doesn't change anything."

"I think the fact that you like Prince is beyond fascinating," I tell her.

"Michael Jackson too. Probably more."

"The King of Pop and Prince. How can I compete with those two?"

"There's a whole lot of things you'd have to compete with in order to be in the Cara Hill world."

"So let me try."

Those blue eyes look sad and serious. I know her answer without even having to hear anything.

I nod. I know when enough is enough. I tried fixing some-one once in my life and that didn't turn out so great. I'm not about to start a rebuilding project again.

"So you have my contact info," I tell her.

"I also have a complimentary 'Redneck Reject' T-shirt, which I will treasure for the rest of my life."

I smile. Even now she's joking around.

There's more I want to say. More I should say. More I should do. But instead, I hold back.

"Merry Christmas, Librarian Girl," I say.

Then I kiss the side of her cheek in a friendly and safe way.

It's the only way I know how to tell her good-bye.

We all knew your father loved Christmas. The day after Thanksgiving, he'd get a tree and drag out all of the decorations from the attic so we could start the monthlong celebration. It wasn't just a holiday for him. It was a special time he never took for granted. Our large extended family getting together on Christmas with everybody bringing their specialty. Turkey, ham, dressing, pecan and pumpkin pies, every dish you can imagine and lots of them. We'd eat and visit all day. And if we ever started to take this day for granted, you know your father—he'd call us out. I love that about him. I love how Christmas meant so much to him.

CHAPTER TWENTY-SIX

Rockin' Around
the Christmas Tree

 *T*t's forty miles from Tulsa to Okmulgee. It's possible I can spend that time stewing in some strange melancholy pining-away-over-Cara sort of thing. But that's ridiculous. We met and had a good time and said good-bye. End. Of. Story.

Happens all the time and I'm used to it.

I grab my phone and check the things I've put on hold. I see several texts that have gone unanswered and several calls that have gone unnoticed.

From Naomi:

> Where are you I've tried calling a dozen times can't you
> at least say hi it's Christmas.

From my manager, Sam Goldberg:

> Happy holidays! Have you decided on any Christmas
> songs?

From my personal assistant, Liz:

> I just saw that your flight got canceled and you're stuck!!
> Did you make it home?

The list goes on. I listen to some voice mails but don't have any desire to make any calls back. I haven't answered any of the fan e-mails for some time, which is unusual for me. But for now, I'm still stranded. For now, I'm still on Christmas break.

For now, I'm still thinking of Cara and can't really start to think of anything else.

Maybe I'll talk to her again sometime. Maybe in the new year. She'll say hello and ask me how Christmas was and it will be very formal and awkward and the beautiful real-ness to our relationship will be gone.

I look at the clock. It's almost noon.

Turn around.

My inner voice must be completely drunk. There's no way I'm turning around. Cara will be gone anyway. She'll be at her parents' house refereeing the chaos and being miserable doing it.

You've still got time. Turn around.

But I keep driving this tiny little car. I don't even want to think about returning it to another micro car rental company. Chances are I'll have to drive several hours to find one.

Just call her, then.

But that's crazy too. There's no need. It's over. It was fun, but it's over and that's that. You have to move on.

Like you moved on after your father passed away? Like you said good-bye?

Suddenly I really don't like talking to myself and thinking out loud. Or thinking at all. I turn up the radio loud and crank an obnoxious pop Christmas song and start driving faster.

That's always how it's gone. For the last thirty-five years of my life.

I'm onstage once again, except this time in the living room surrounded by those who genuinely love me. My sisters and their families are all there as I hug Momma and give her a kiss on the cheek.

"Miss me?"

"Worried you weren't gonna make it," she says.

"I'm here."

The wild gang surrounds me with hugs and laughter and questions. I smile and hear how they're doing and yet I can't help but think of her. The figure doused with coffee rushing into the men's room.

"So all the flights were canceled?" Karen asks me. "You had to drive yourself?"

I think of sitting next to her while the plane bounced around and for a moment I held her hand and I felt okay.

"I had some traveling companions."

I picture her arriving in the bar all made up and still not having any idea of who I was. I can see her I-can't-believe-this moment as I play the piano for the drunken, stranded patrons.

"So what was her name? Who was she? Come on, I know you have a story."

Anne always loves a good story, especially when it has some humor in it, like pretty much every one of my stories.

I see the Amtrak train and the small confined space we sat in and I recall just watching her sleeping. Until, of course, we ran into Santa the pizza deliveryman.

"So where is this mystery woman?" Becky asks me.

I recall that ride with her mean cousin and then stumbling upon the tiniest car in the world, only to get stranded inside it.

"She could've come over for dinner," Momma says.

I see one of the three Christmas trees in the house and all the decorations on it. I can smell a turkey and sweet potatoes and dressing and pecan pies all waiting to be eaten. Somewhere in this house is a hermit cake that has my name written all over it.

Then I remember that moment in the snow-covered car outside the gas station that really could have been anywhere. We could have been strangers in Moscow stuck inside some small snowbound room, huddled up and ready for a moment. A moment where we kiss and I feel more free and alive than I've felt in a long time. In a very long time.

"So what happened?" Anne wants to know.

I see us in that guest bedroom, looking and knowing and then letting it go. I hear us talking and can hear us laughing and I love the way it sounds.

"I think he's not gonna tell us," Becky says.

Then I see us surrounded by a sweet family of five on Christmas morning and feeling as natural as I do now.

I'm not sure how to describe all of this to them, because *noth-*

ing really did happen. I met a quirky girl and she helped me get home and we kissed and we almost kissed again and we shared some moments and we laughed a lot and then we said good-bye.

"It's almost time to eat," Momma says.

"Then we have a surprise later," Karen says.

I look at the kids running around and smell the meal waiting for me and see the presents we're about to open and something doesn't feel right.

How does it feel, Heath?

I recall what she said.

I'm bummed for having to go home.

I'm a fool. A tool. I'm the idiot in all of my songs. Again.

"I have to leave," I tell them.

"What?"

"Where are you going?"

"You just got here."

"Are you okay?"

I can't tell them now because there's too much to sum up and too much time has already passed.

"I can't . . . Look, all of you sit down and eat and enjoy yourselves . . . I know, don't ask, just don't wait, don't stop anything you're doing . . . I'll be back."

I grab the coat I just took off and don't even slip it back on. I start to head back out the door, back to get this wonderful girl who I'm letting escape my life, when all of a sudden I'm pulled back into the room.

Becky has one of my arms and Karen has the other.

"Uh-uh, boy," Becky says. "You're staying right here."

"We waited long enough for you to get here," Karen says. "We're all starving and we're not waiting another minute."

I know it's a hopeless situation. They'll pry me out of my micro car if they have to. There are three of them and I'm only one. And I'm not counting their husbands or kids either.

"Look, guys, I'm trying to have a Hallmark moment here," I tell them. "I'm trying to get the right girl. Just wait till you meet her."

"We can meet her," Anne tells me. "Just not *now*. Right now, we're having dinner."

"And you're staying put," Becky says.

"*And* you're doing the dishes afterward," Karen says.

I look at the men in the room and shake my head. "And you guys wonder why I stay away."

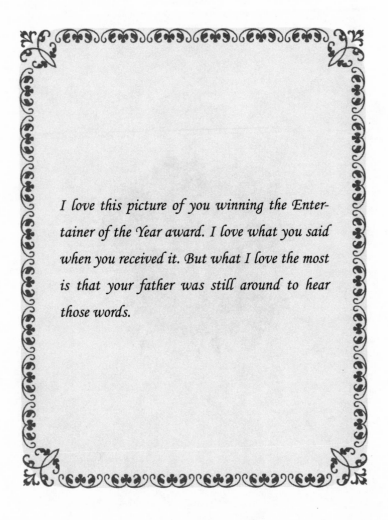

I love this picture of you winning the Entertainer of the Year award. I love what you said when you received it. But what I love the most is that your father was still around to hear those words.

CHAPTER TWENTY-SEVEN

It's the Most Wonderful Time of the Year

It's nice to just blend in for a while. At the crowded table, with my sisters and their husbands and kids, everyone is talking at once, telling stories and passing dishes across the table. My sisters might love to give me a hard time, but they also love to cook. If I stuck around here long enough, I'd gain a hundred pounds simply from eating all the time. Between the kids talking and yelling and running around and everybody getting a dozen different selections on their plates, conversation flows from one disjointed topic to another. The nice thing is the topic is not about me. They're used to Heath. The little brother. Or Uncle Heath. That guy out there, the name everybody knows, isn't sitting at the dining room table.

"Have some more," Karen tells me even though I've already eaten twice as much as my trainer would've suggested.

I'm not gonna mention my trainer. If I do I'll just get subjected to the abuse I know so well.

Momma has made both a turkey and a ham. I guess she felt bad that I didn't have ham yesterday, so she made another one. There's her own secret recipe for sweet potatoes, and they're as evil and addictive as crack. I get some of Anne's homemade stuffing that has a strangely awesome combo of nuts and berries in it. There's also Karen's crazy broccoli cauliflower cheese concoction that also might produce the need for food rehab.

"This is amazing, everybody," I say, like some stranger who knocked on the door and was allowed to wine and dine with these wonderful folks.

At one point, Karen shares a memory of Dad from last year (and the year before and the year before that), trying to get the camera to work to take a picture of everybody and being unable to do it. The way Karen describes it is classic, making everybody howl with laughter. I am literally so tired and happy drunk that it takes me a minute to notice the tears lining my cheeks.

"He was crazy for never buying a decent camera or tripod," I say. "The photos he took were the absolute worst."

"Dreadful," Karen says.

"Oh, they were terrible," Becky says.

We keep talking and laughing and I sneak a peek at Momma. She's smiling too but has tears in her eyes. I don't think those are happy tears.

She looks at me and I know exactly what she's thinking.

I know I need to be here. Not for my sake, but for hers.

*   *   *

"Y'all already know I have something special for you, but at least you don't know what it is," Momma says after we've spent the past hour opening presents.

She has saved the best for last. My sisters tell Momma they don't know what she's talking about, but she just rolls her eyes.

"I've never been able to keep anything from you girls, starting when you were two years old."

"What about me?" I ask.

"We could move to another state and you'd be oblivious to it," she says to a round of laughter.

"That's unfair," I say amidst all the noise. "But true."

"Ben and David—can you boys get the presents in my bedroom?"

Two of my teenage nephews go get them for their grandmother. Karen gives me a look, as if to say, *Here we go.* We've all known that something big was going to happen. There was no way we were going to go through Christmas without stopping and having a moment of reflection and then, surely, complete and total emotional bedlam.

The boys come back carrying large wrapped gifts that look like boxes containing laptop computers.

Momma got us all iPads! Or maybe record players.

The whole family is circled around the tree in the family room, and the four of us are sitting near Momma, close to it. One of the toddlers is roaming around, but otherwise everybody is watching, wondering what these final presents are going to be. It feels heavy, like some kind of serious memento Momma has given us.

She stands up.

Oh, boy, she's getting ready to make a speech. The woman who usually says less than more.

"I know this is the first Christmas we've celebrated without your father, and y'all know just how hard that is. For all of us."

Anne is the first to go down, starting to cry. I'm about to say something funny and witty to acknowledge this, but I decide to stay quiet. Probably best.

Momma looks so beautiful, her face at peace and her demeanor calm and quiet.

"I wanted to do something like this for a long time. I just—I never got around to it. But after Paul left us, I thought I better get on it. Not because I suddenly had more time. We *make* time for the important things in this life. This was important. I wanted all of you to know just how important you are."

For a moment, I watch Karen and Anne and Becky all glancing around, waiting for the other to start.

"Well, go ahead, open them up. All of you."

I rip off the gold wrapping paper and then find a box inside. I'm the first to open it up.

Inside is a dark brown leather photo album with the words THIS IS YOUR LIFE stitched on the front.

"Momma!" Karen hollers.

Becky and Anne react in a similar way as they see their own photo albums and begin to go through them.

I open the first page and see a big picture of myself, this chunky, happy baby wearing a Christmas outfit sitting next to the tree. Momma's neat handwriting is on the page next to the photo.

You were only six months old when you celebrated your first Christmas. I remember rocking you to

sleep that Christmas Eve and singing soft Christmas
carols to you. How could I ever imagine those songs
would inspire you to become the man you are today?

A wave of unexpected emotion hits me. I knew the gift would be meaningful, but the amount of time and energy that went into this . . .

"This is incredible, Mom," Becky says, putting it down and going to hug her.

I quickly leaf through the pages and see photos of me throughout the years around Christmastime. Each page has a similar note and a similar memory attached to it.

You probably don't remember spending Christmas
Eve in the hospital, but I do . . .
Those little curly locks of yours made me want to
grow your hair long . . .
Your sisters loved you . . .

I quickly wipe my cheeks. Ridiculous crying about a Christmas present, but here I am, doing it.

"Your father and I had talked about doing this for years. But after he got so sick, I couldn't bear doing it. But after he died, I couldn't bear *not* doin' it. He would have wanted us to celebrate Christmas and to celebrate each other."

Everybody is surrounding us, looking at the fancy photo albums. Karen and Becky and Anne are talking and laughing and thanking Momma, but I'm speechless because I'm almost paralyzed with feeling. Good feelings and bad and strange ones and ones I've never felt or have forgotten about.

"No matter what happens, y'all are the best gifts God ever gave us," Momma says. "We love you and always will. That's what your father would've said. That's what he still thinks now, looking down on us."

Oh, boy.

The tears start a-flowin' and the hugs start a-comin'. I'd jump up and run out of the room if I wasn't surrounded by family on all sides.

I don't bother reading every word Momma wrote. I'll have time to read through all of it, to soak it in and get emotional and look back on my life.

For now, I just put the photo album down and go to hug my mother.

"Thank you," I whisper in her ear. "I love you."

"I know you do. Just don't ever go and forget that, you hear?"

She kisses me on the cheek.

An hour later, when I finally manage to read through the whole photo album, I get to the final page and then realize what I have to do.

I need to take my mother's advice. I need to honor this gift she gave us.

This time I don't announce I'm leaving but simply get my coat and slip out the front door.

I'm doing exactly what she said for me to do. I'm doing it today. Doing it now.

I'm going to do something for myself, something for my life and not my career.

I'm going to get Cara and bring her back here.

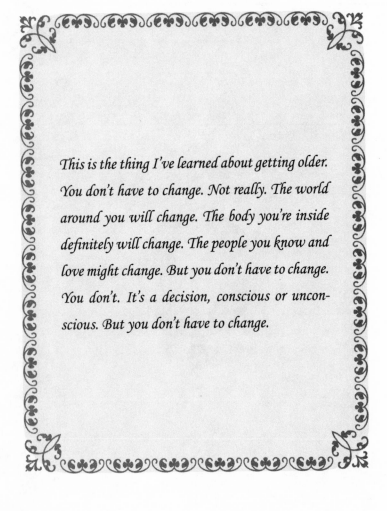

This is the thing I've learned about getting older. You don't have to change. Not really. The world around you will change. The body you're inside definitely will change. The people you know and love might change. But you don't have to change. You don't. It's a decision, conscious or unconscious. But you don't have to change.

CHAPTER TWENTY-EIGHT

Cool Yule

"*H*eath?"

Momma is standing by the window of my car and suddenly seems like a giant. She's surely checking to see if I've lost my mind. I roll the window down. The afternoon sky is somewhere stuck behind thick clouds above.

"I'm fine, Momma."

"What's going on?"

There's one thing I know about Momma. There's no way to BS her.

"It's a girl."

"A girl?"

I nod. I chose that word carefully. I didn't say a woman or a chick or a friend or a lady I just met. I mentioned a girl.

"You really like her?"

"I think so," I say.

"So why didn't you bring her by?"

"I tried."

"No, you didn't."

I'm my mother. The same drive and the same competitive nature and the same fire burning inside of me came mostly from her. She might smile and be polite and charming and never seem assertive at all, but Momma knows what she wants. And she gets it.

"I got afraid," I say.

"You? Afraid? What were you afraid of?"

"I didn't want to repeat past mistakes."

Her look reflects wisdom, those dark eyes surely knowing what I'm referring to.

"Not every woman is going to turn out like Reilly."

Some are too broken to fix. But not Cara. Not the woman that helped me find my way back home.

"I'm going back to Tulsa to get her," I say with total confidence.

"Think she'll come with you this time?"

I nod. "Yeah. If not, I'll kidnap her."

"Come back. Soon. Okay?"

"I want her to meet everybody before the day becomes night. So, yeah—I'll be coming back."

I look at the house behind her and it looks like something from a Hallmark movie. The snow hangs on the trees and the Christmas lights make the snow shimmer. The steps leading to the door look inviting, calling you to go inside.

"You really outdid yourself this year," I tell her.

"I didn't decorate the house."

"No—you inspired it. That's even better."

She smiles and kisses my cheek.

"Hurry up. But don't look too desperate."

"What kind of statement is that? Do I look desperate?"

"A bit."

I shake my head. "That inspires confidence. Good-bye, Momma."

"Heath?"

I suddenly see a look I haven't wanted to see in a while, a look I've been avoiding. It's the same sad and empty look I saw on Momma's face at Dad's funeral.

"Don't keep running away from this place. Just because he's gone doesn't mean the rest of us are."

Normally I might argue with her or make a joke, but now I simply smile and nod.

"Okay."

She's right. Momma usually is.

Don't look too desperate.

It's time to be the hero. Time to be the lonesome cowboy. Time to be the loving country fool that I am. It takes me a couple of minutes to find a good song, but I find one and crank it up. It's loud and this tiny car might be only as big as my boot, but it still can crank the sound. So I blast this song out and feel the soul vibe redneck pulse back in my soul.

I'm flying and I'm running to my future.

I want someone I can be myself around, really let my guard down with. I want someone to want me for my heart, my soul, and not my name or my bank account. I want someone who makes me laugh and surprises me, who can be both tender and tough. I want someone who lives in Oklahoma and has never started really, truly living her life but rather feels trapped the same way a famous country star might feel.

I want Cara Hill.

And I'm racing to her, hoping that she might want me. I'm racing until . . .

Suddenly everything slows down. Like, *way* down.

I get behind a minivan that's seriously driving at about ten miles an hour. This is the winding road that heads to the highway. I can't pass, but then again, I could *run* and pass this guy driving. It's ridiculous. I start to pass, but then he speeds up. Then he slows down again.

The song I was blasting ends and a slower Christmas song continues to squelch my once-swelling mood.

"Come on, Grampa!"

When I begin to pass, I realize this micro car I'm driving has the acceleration of a turtle. I'm glad this is a green car, but right now all I'm seeing is red.

On a flat stretch of road, I finally am able to coast past the minivan. As I do, I notice the driver.

He's got a white beard and is wearing a Santa cap.

Come on.

I actually slow down to get a look at Santa behind the wheel when I notice a truck heading my way. I slam on the brakes and jerk back into my lane.

Santa has followed me and he's up to his old tricks again.

This is unbelievable.

I keep riding his tail, but suddenly I don't want to pass him. I'm afraid he'll show up again. And again. And again. Jolly ol' Saint Nick, who is neither jolly nor a saint.

I reach the exit for the highway and take it while Santa Claus keeps driving his minivan. Heading to go find Donner and Blixen probably.

The road is my familiar friend. The scenery, my sweet sister. The silence, my only source of sanity. I drive and keep wondering what I'm going to say to Cara. What kind of grand entrance I'm going to make.

The utter quiet bothers me, so I turn on the radio again. And search. And search until I find a song I bet Cara would love.

I think something is different inside of me, but I don't know exactly how to define it. All I can think about is a hundred different maybe's.

Maybe it is my turn now.

Maybe I'm finally ready to hold someone's hand and not let it go.

Maybe it's time to stop letting the Heath Sawyer that everyone thinks I am replace the real me.

Maybe I'm ready to stand still for a while and to allow someone else in my life. To start to sacrifice something for someone else instead of everyone sacrificing everything for me.

Maybe.

You're not ready for someone else and especially not for someone like her.

I know that because it doesn't fit and doesn't make sense.

"Home" by Michael Bublé starts to play, and somehow I imagine Cara listening to it and getting what I'm thinking now that I'm listening to it thinking about her.

That's crazy.

Or maybe that's a beautiful thing.

What if's fill my mind.

What's wrong with me?

I'm just tired. And hungover. And ready to be home. Ready to be . . .

Truly home.

A place where I can be myself, and I can joke and I can feel free to just be anything I want to be and not have to be on and not have to worry about what people expect . . .

Exactly like I feel with Cara.

Whoa.

This isn't supposed to happen. I'm supposed to be arrested or spotted at a gentleman's club or maybe in the news about breaking up with some model. Right? Isn't that my persona? That's the perception and the whole pop culture star-crazed world.

Cara reminds me of the dreamy symphony and smooth vocal blasting through the car speakers.

I know what I have to do now. And normally I never think twice.

I hear "The Christmas Song" come on and realize this is *my* Christmas song. Maybe Yuletide carols are being sung by a choir somewhere, and maybe folks are dressed like Eskimos somewhere. That's all fine and dandy, but at this moment all I'm thinking about is that crazy, quirky woman I took a trip with halfway across America.

I'm the turkey and she's the mistletoe. And both help to make the season bright. Right?

Santa's on his way, Cara. And he's only bringing one goodie with him on his sleigh.

His heart.

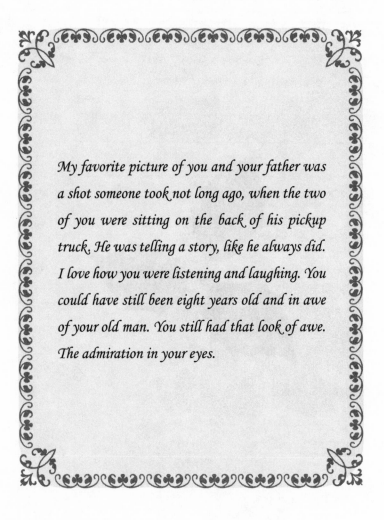

My favorite picture of you and your father was a shot someone took not long ago, when the two of you were sitting on the back of his pickup truck. He was telling a story, like he always did. I love how you were listening and laughing. You could have still been eight years old and in awe of your old man. You still had that look of awe. The admiration in your eyes.

CHAPTER TWENTY-NINE

Merry Christmas to You

I bet Cara's not even going to be there.

I pull up to the cream-colored one-story house, and it looks the same as it did when I left it. A wreath hangs on the door. I turn off the motor and sit for a minute to get myself together. I imagine myself like some kid heading to the doorway of the hottest girl in school, knowing he's only going to find rejection.

A few days ago you played Madison Freaking Square Garden, and look at you now, you pathetic fool.

Only women can turn men into boys.

I find myself standing on her stoop. I'm not sure whether to ring the doorbell or knock and then suddenly the door opens as if I'm some Jedi Master who's played a mind trick on it.

"Heath?"

She's wearing a faded, oversized sweatshirt and jeans. Her hair is messy, as if she's been sleeping.

She's never looked more beautiful.

"I made a mistake," I say.

"Did you leave something behind?"

"Yeah. You."

She has the look of a woman in shock. Not surprise but shock. It's strange to see because you don't see this every day. I might as well be standing out here telling her she won the million-dollar sweepstakes.

"Obviously you're not going anywhere anytime soon, are you?"

For a moment, she shivers. It's cold and I'm the only one who's wearing a jacket. "Come on in."

I follow her to her living room. It's a little sparse, but warm, a bit modern. Two blue sofas sit on opposite sides of the room, with a couple of chairs along another side. Some family pictures are framed and hang on the wall. The television is on and I see it's paused in midmovie.

"What is that?" I ask.

"Nothing." She goes to find the remote.

"Is that Hugh Grant?"

"No."

"Yeah, it is. What movie is that?"

She turns it off and sits down on the couch, but then turns her head to the side and rolls her eyes. *Love Actually.*

"Is that a Christmas movie?"

"Does Bing Crosby sing?" she says.

"Okay, then. I take it you're a fan."

She nods. I notice the glass of red wine on the coffee table. Then the sliver of turkey on a plate.

"Is *this* your Christmas dinner?"

"No. This? No. Absolutely not."

"Then what's going on?" I ask.

She tightens her lips, then pulls her legs together toward her chest and wraps her arms around them. "I don't want to face them. Not today. Not tonight."

"Your family?"

"All of them. I don't. I can't. I won't."

I nod. "So that's why I'm here, then. Come home with me."

"Heath, didn't we already talk about this?"

"No, actually, I don't think we did. I think you talked to me about it. About what you think is going to happen and how it's going to be and all this nonsense. My only problem—my big problem—was that I didn't say anything back. I just let you go believin' all that."

"It's true."

"No, it's not. How in the world do you know? You know me as well as a tabloid magazine."

"That bad?"

"Okay, more than that, but still. You have— How do you know how things will work out? Has this ever happened to you before?"

"I'm drinking wine and eating turkey and watching *Love Actually* on Christmas. Yeah, this happens to me, like, all the time."

I love the bite in her sarcasm.

"This is new to me," I tell her.

"Really? Do you really mean that?"

"Yeah, I do. What—why don't you believe that?"

"I don't—I have no idea. I don't know how your world works."

"'My world'? You know—we're from the same state. That counts for something. My mother is going to love that."

"Yeah, right. Like you told her about me."

"I did," I say. "I told them all. I got there and realized something was missing. Or more like *someone*."

She shakes her head. "Did someone drug you or something?"

"Maybe."

I see that smile. "I'm going to wake up and realize I ate the whole turkey and drank the whole bottle of wine and this is just a dream."

"Why don't you grab that turkey and come back home with me? I'll drink enough wine for the both of us."

That smile isn't leaving those lips. And all I want to do is kiss her again, but I'm not going to. Not now. Not yet. I'm going to wait and see how this plays out.

"Your family is going to just love me," she says with disbelief.

"They will. As long as you act like yourself."

"And how's that?"

"Be honest and real and funny and . . . and act like you did when you first met me."

"No, I can't." She folds her arms over her chest in the oversized sweatshirt. "I know things are easy for you, but look—I just can't. It's just not that easy for me."

I sit on a chair facing her as she sits on the couch. She doesn't look like she's going to budge.

"Do you know why I was so late in traveling home? I wasn't gonna go back. I kept putting it off and putting it off. And it was because I didn't want to go back and deal with things. I didn't want to go back home because I wasn't sure how it'd be without my father."

"But you did."

I nod. "You want to know a story nobody has ever heard? Not even CMT?"

"What's CMT?"

I can only sigh. "Girl, you gotta know a little more about country. It's Country Music Television. Anyway, about ten years ago, after a series of mishaps and mistakes and nonsense, I decided to scrap my dreams and come back to Oklahoma. I wanted to do something—anything—other than pursue a musical career. And shortly after I was back, my father took me out fishing. And it was there he gave me advice that changed my life."

"Let me guess," Cara says, brushing the hair out of her eyes. "He told you to not give up on your dreams, to keep at it and you'd eventually find success."

"No." I move over to sit next to her. I take her hand. "No. He knew I'd already done that. I'd released a couple of albums by then. But my career was stalling and I was tired. I remember that day with Dad well. It was the middle of the day and nothing was biting and everything around us was so silent. So peaceful. I can still see him right next to me, so healthy and alive."

I haven't told anybody this, not even Momma.

Cara waits for me to continue. For a moment I wonder if I can. But I feel her touch and see her tender face and know I can.

"Dad told me that anybody can follow a dream. The important thing—the thing that defines us—is what happens when that dream fails. The world makes it easy to give up on dreams. To settle for something less when we know there can be something far better. Too many people let the dreams dry up and fade away."

"Dreams are dangerous," Cara says.

I can see the fear and the sadness on her face.

"Dreams are gifts. Complacency is the dangerous thing."

I see those blue eyes land on me and study me for a moment. "You really did come back to pick me up and bring me back to your house, didn't you?"

"Of course."

She shakes her head, looks down, then laughs. "Do you realize how crazy attracted I am to you right now?"

"That . . . uh, no."

"Do you realize I'm about two seconds away from just jumping on top of you and going crazy?" she says.

I think I start to say something, but then it happens again. Once again I'm turned into a boy who doesn't quite know what to say.

"But I'm not going to do that, out of respect for you and your family," she says, standing up and then walking out of the room. "Give me ten minutes, okay?"

My mind is still twenty seconds behind.

Ten minutes? Ten minutes to slip into something more comfortable and put on some Sade?

"I'm not showing up at your house in a sweatshirt," she says.

Ah . . .

"Okay."

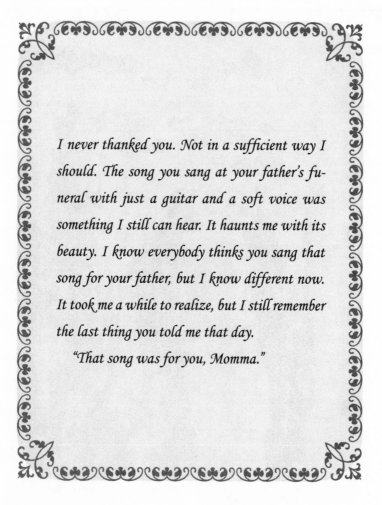

I never thanked you. Not in a sufficient way I should. The song you sang at your father's funeral with just a guitar and a soft voice was something I still can hear. It haunts me with its beauty. I know everybody thinks you sang that song for your father, but I know different now. It took me a while to realize, but I still remember the last thing you told me that day.

"That song was for you, Momma."

CHAPTER THIRTY

The Very Best Time of the Year

I'm almost getting used to driving this micro car. The same way I'm getting used to not feeling my lower half below my belt buckle. This isn't a vehicle. It's a mousetrap without the cheese.

"We're almost there," I tell Cara.

"Can I ask you something?"

I nod, but then feel her tug my arm.

"Pull over for a second."

I look at her and then look ahead. We're driving down a narrow country road with nothing around except the fading sun in the distance. "What's wrong?"

"Just—right up there—the edge of the road."

I'm not sure what she wants, but I'm willing to oblige her. I pull over and turn the motor off. So far we haven't spoken about anything too deep or heavy, which has been fine with me. There was enough of that back at her house. But Cara's got a look on her face that says she wants to plunge into those deep and heavy waters.

"You gotta tell me something, okay? Maybe not a promise because—because we're maybe not at the promise stage. But a semipromise."

"Um . . . okay."

I have no idea where this is going.

"I don't want—no, let me say I can't—end up finding myself down the road taking care of you. Okay?"

"Okay."

"No, no, no. That's a weak response. Tell me you hear what I'm saying."

"Yeah, I do."

"I don't want to replace this burden I have with my family with another burden."

I nod, then take her hand. "The last thing I want is to be a burden. But I'll be honest. You're good at taking care of people."

"That's my problem."

"It won't be with me. Okay? I want to learn what it's like to take care of someone. And I think I found that somebody. Right now I just want to bring you back home and have everything feel natural. Casual."

"I am meeting your family. There's a certain amount of terror in that."

"More than riding with your cousin? I don't know—that was pretty dang terrifying."

She laughs and that's a good thing. She's good at taking

care of people and I'm good at making them laugh. Not sure how those two things complement each other, but right now I don't care.

"Look, Cara—this is all I know. This is all I can tell you. I've spent a long time running away and a long time running toward this music thing. It's been pretty much everything. When I met you, I finally enjoyed stopping for a while. It was nice. And I don't—I can't—just run away again. It's like—it's like when you write a song. You know when you have a hit. You just know."

I pause for a minute to let her respond, but she doesn't. So I open my mouth to fill up the silence again. Like I always do.

"Look, I'll just be honest here, all I know—"

"Okay," Cara interrupts.

"What?"

"Okay. We can go."

"And we're all good?"

She smiles. Then laughs. Then shakes her head. "Oh, yeah. We're good. More than good, in fact. Really, really good."

Maybe something I said finally worked. Like a lyric that you come up with that finally fits and you just know the song is going to be a hit.

Sometimes I get lucky.

Then again, that's the story of every single guy I've ever known.

It's funny watching my family meet Cara. It's not what's said—they all say the same thing you'd think they'd say. The "Nice to meet you" and the "Glad you could come by" and all that polite stuff. But I can see it on their faces.

My sisters, of course, are the best in terms of expressions. They've been used to seeing some of the women I've brought around. A couple of them I've already apologized for. I'm a man. No shame. That's been my excuse.

Up to now.

But this is different.

Anne lights up and hugs Cara as if she's known her for years. "Look at you!"

The family was just unwrapping leftovers and reheating the holiday meal, so we've arrived just in time. My mother greets Cara with a hug and also with attempts to feed her.

Becky gives me a look that says, *Why didn't you tell us she was a normal girl?* after she talks to Cara and thanks her for helping get me back home.

My eldest sister's expression is the best, however. Karen's always been my second mother of sorts. She is the one to both baby me and scold me, to remind me of where I come from and who I am at the core. She keeps looking at Cara with a smile. She almost looks proud of me.

"Our brother should have told us more about you," Karen says to Cara. "But he will. Oh, he will."

Cara is suddenly the center of attention instead of the caregiver. It amuses me and also makes me wonder.

They all like her.

Of course they do.

She fits in here with them.

Of course she does.

So what's this mean, then?

But I don't want to think that far ahead. I'm taking this a day at a time. Maybe an hour at a time. I might be enjoying everything and life is smooth sailing and then suddenly I might hit the pizza deliveryman with a train. Life can be unpredictable and make no sense. And maybe, just for once, I should try to appreciate everything I have.

I laugh at the whole insanity of everything that has happened to lead to this moment around my momma's table. Cara catches me and asks if I'm laughing at her.

"Yeah, I am."

"Just ignore him," Becky says to Cara. "We all do."

"And *that* is exactly the sort of love I get around here."

But we all know better. Especially me.

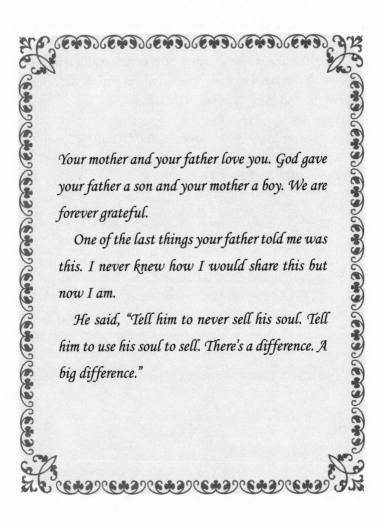

Your mother and your father love you. God gave your father a son and your mother a boy. We are forever grateful.

One of the last things your father told me was this. I never knew how I would share this but now I am.

He said, "Tell him to never sell his soul. Tell him to use his soul to sell. There's a difference. A big difference."

CHAPTER THIRTY-ONE

Winter Wonderland

*S*ome things just fit. Like Cara sitting next to me on this old couch I've told Momma to get rid of but never gotten her to be able to do it. The glow of the Christmas tree in the corner lights the room. We've been sitting here talking with everybody and watching while one by one they went to bed. The family has all dwindled down and left us alone in front of a slow-burning fireplace that simmers and has no plans of going out.

"So what's next for you?"

"I don't know," I tell Cara.

"No big world tour? No album plans?"

"I'm supposed to have a list of songs to my manager in the next week for a possible Christmas album."

"Oh, dear," she says.

"What?"

"Now *that's* a Christmas album I want to hear."

"Maybe you will."

"Okay, then," Cara says, joking around with her attitude and tone.

"I've got an idea for the Christmas album. An original Christmas song. It's something I've been thinking about and avoiding for a long time. A song about my father."

"How's it go?"

"I'm calling it 'Lost in Christmas.'"

"Is that 'in' or 'on'?"

"You did halfway inspire that title," I admit.

"So do you have any lyrics? Is that bad luck to ask?"

"Nah—it's fine. Let me see—I have a few lines." I think of the melody for a moment. "'I've been runnin' in the snow, but can't see the tracks I've left behind. I know a storm's a-comin', but won't let that change my mind.' That's just a verse. And then here's the chorus. 'A stocking full of memories, a gift-wrapped Okie sky. I'm lost in Christmas, 'cause I can't say good-bye.'"

She tightens up her arms and shakes her entire body.

"What?"

"I just got goose bumps. And I know that's such a cliché, but I can't help saying it, and it's totally true."

"No, you didn't."

"Yes, I did. I swear. Now, if you make it a pop song, I'll absolutely love it."

"No respect," I say.

"You need to write and record that song, Heath. You have to."

I just look at her and nod. I can hear the emphasis in her voice, the *you need to make sure you listen to me right now* tone.

"Wait a minute," she says, sitting up as if she's suddenly had a brilliant idea. "Did you get your family any Christmas gifts? Any really bad gift cards?"

I shake my head. "I told them I was going to on the way home, but . . ."

"So write *that* song and write it for them. For all of them. How cool of a Christmas present would that be?"

"That'd be pretty cool. Of course, they might not get it until spring."

Cara smiles. "Just add this to your to-do list."

"I don't want to think about all of the work I have to do," I say. "I just want to think about now."

"So what's next for now?"

"Don't tell me you're thinking about leaving?"

Cara only shakes her head. "No. I just think we need some way to end this story."

"It's only just started."

"But Christmas is over and I still don't know quite what to do with my Willie Nelson album."

"He'll grow on you. I promise."

"You absolutely sure about that?" She looks at me with soft, safe eyes, the kind I can imagine looking into a million more times.

"Oh, yeah. You'll love him. He may let you down sometimes, but you'll forgive him. You gotta forgive him."

Cara raises her eyes. "And why's that?"

"Because he'll forgive you. That's how it works, right?"

"Oh, really?"

"Yes. And sometimes he even sings Michael Jackson."

I can see her confusion. "Who are we talking about again?"

"Willie Nelson, obviously. He recorded a beautiful cover of

a Michael Jackson song, 'She's Out of My Life.' See—sometimes the two roads *do* meet."

"If that's where they meet, well . . . that's not so good. I mean—'She's out of my life'? Not a lot of hope there."

"Okay, well—LeAnn Rimes covered Prince. Pretty rockin' rendition of 'Purple Rain.'"

"That's a little better."

I lean into her, not taking my eyes off her, watching the smile linger on her lips.

"If we were a Prince song, you know how things would end."

"We are *not* a Prince song."

"Okay. Just sayin'."

"We're more of a . . . a Burl Ives song."

"Ouch," I say.

"So how does this song end in the country world?"

"You act like you're from L.A. or New York or somewhere like that," I say. "You should know, Oklahoma girl."

"I'm just asking," Cara says.

"How about this? A guy and a girl meet in an unlikely way. They're definitely different, but somehow that works. Somehow they make each other better. And they find themselves at the end of one song and the beginning of another. And the great thing with that—the beauty of it all—is that they can keep creating song after song if they want. Forget the albums— who buys albums anymore? They can keep making song after song and letting each one be different and unique and meaningful. They don't have to fit in a box or a genre or a holiday. They simply have to fit into the two of them. That's all that matters."

"Wow." Cara looks astonished.

"What?"

"That was a mouthful."

"I can keep talking if you want—"

She silences me with a kiss. A soft kiss, with passion just below the surface. It's the kind of kiss that songs are written about, the kind that Christmas stories begin and end with.

I think—no, I know—I'm finally back home.

And I hope home is here to stay.

Every day is a gift. Don't blink and wish you could go back ten years and do something. Do it today. Do it now. There are things I'd like to say to your father. Things I would have loved to do over. But that's life. Sometimes the only way you learn is the hard way. Life can hurt, but it's what we do with the hurt that matters.

These pictures and these memories—they will always be a part of me like you're a part of me. No matter what happens, you will always be my little boy. And this will always be your home. Don't run too far. And don't stay away too long.

I love you. Merry Christmas.

Lost in Christmas

A CHRISTMAS ALBUM BY HEATH SAWYER

1. "Mele Kalikimaka"
2. "Cool Yule" (Oklahama Style)
3. "Rockin' Around the Christmas Tree"
4. "Christmastime Is Here"
5. "2000 Miles"
6. "Step into Christmas"
7. "Silver Bells" (For my agent)
8. "Another Lonely Christmas" (For my Prince-loving fan)
9. "Merry Christmas to You"
10. "That Was the Worst Christmas Ever!"
11. "Here Comes Santa Claus"
12. "A Holly Jolly Christmas"
13. "Christmas Lights"
14. "Lost in Christmas" (For you, Pop)